DEAD PIANO

BOOKS BY

HENRY VAN DYKE:

Dead Piano   (*1 9 7 1*)

Blood of Strawberries   (*1 9 6 8*)

Ladies of the Rachmaninoff Eyes   (*1 9 6 5*)

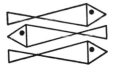

DEAD PIANO

HENRY VAN DYKE

FARRAR, STRAUS & GIROUX (New York)

FOR

EDWARD McGEHEE,

PEG, AND MARY

DEAD PIANO

(1)

ALTHOUGH THE silver needles performed acrobatics in and out of the blue wool on her lap, Olga Blake was not really knitting. Whenever her fingers and wrists faltered, she scarcely noticed the tangle that disrupted the seductive, mindless rhythm. She looked at it, the formless yarn hanging from the needles, and she looked at her quick fingers as they made purl and plain stitches, but her mind was focused beyond the point of the design, beyond immediate concern for her handiwork. Occasionally she lifted her eyes from her lap and glanced across the living room at her daughter, picking at bits and pieces of a sonatina on the piano, or sometimes she shot a glance toward the newspaper in front of her husband's face, but more often, when she disengaged herself from the knitting in her lap, she glanced toward the foyer, toward the front door, and she listened.

Again, it was only the leaves—crisp, withered leaves slipping over one another and scrabbling upon the stones of the garden wall. Autumn was early and aggressive that year in St. Albans, that September of 1968, and there seemed, although it was only the eighth, little chance for an Indian summer; the leaves, instead of gently changing into russet and amber, yellow and red, had quickly turned brown and crisp, irritable and ugly. Olga heard them now, scraping like footsteps on the garden stones and upon the gravel in the driveway. Or had *that* been a leaf, she wondered, this time even stopping the clicking of her needles so that she could hear better, could better assess the exact nature of the movement outside. But almost immediately the night wind rose again and sent the dying leaves scurrying into scratchy whispers, blurring her attempt to analyze the sound.

Had Olga heard a strange or undefined noise in almost any other part of the New York area, she would not have given it a second thought, but in St. Albans —at least in her particular part of St. Albans—the wide streets were quiet and gentle: around her streets she could distinguish the chirp of a blue jay from the quick note of a cardinal; she could tell by the crush of the tires on the pavement whether it was a milk truck or a mail truck passing. Her house with its long lawn and small rose garden was more than forty minutes away from Manhattan's constant noise and many blocks away from the bustling that could always be heard in the borough of Queens. She had become accustomed to labeling all sounds, defining all noise. It came again, that footstep that perhaps wasn't a footstep, and this time she decided, but without honest relief, that it was

merely the wind whipping the plastic umbrella trimmings out on the lawn by the bird bath. Summer was
over. She would take the umbrellas down first thing in
the morning.

Olga Blake could almost have passed for forty and she
could almost have passed for white, the one depending
on the time of day and the other on the company
present. Oddly enough, it was at the end of the day that
she seemed to flower, appeared to be forty, or even
younger, rather than her true forty-seven years. For
although she often lamented the "ruination" of her
nerves and complained about "tension," she, deny it
as she would, thrived on a regulated state of chaos,
flourished in controlled turmoil. The tension, which
she protested she could not bear, enlivened and quick-
ened her responses; the irritation of her nerves actually
added piquancy to her beauty.

It was usually in the evening when Finley, her husband, returned from the hospital or his clinic that her
nerves were in their worst state (brought on by vacuous
household duties and silent war with Lucille, the day
maid), and usually it took only the slightest contretemps
with Sophie, her seventeen-year-old daughter, to make
her as taut as stretched tinsel (a condition that Sophie
considered her mother's normal state). Sophie could
find no added zest, no heightened youth or beauty, in
her mother's countenance and demeanor; Sophie, at

seventeen, could not apply these attributes to anyone who was forty-seven, an age that in her mind was, if not actually ancient, at least very advanced.

Olga had never tried passing for white, although she knew that her own father, when she was still a young girl, had disappeared from her life under the protective shield of his flaxen hair and his pale skin. A Scottish and Cree Indian ancestry, from a muddled past, had also left its mark on Olga: she was often taken for an Algerian, or a sun-tanned Latin, or for almost anything except Negro. Taxi drivers were the worst offenders in mistaking her race. Apparently, a glance in a rearview mirror was not enough for the driver to see that she was not white. As recently as two weeks ago, when she had given her address on Adelaide Lane, the driver had clucked his tongue and shaken his head to establish sympathetic complicity before he said, "Ain't it a shame —that neighborhood . . . it use to be the swankiest section in all of St. Albans. Jeez, now look at it. Niggers moving in right and left."

It was cowardice and despair that made Olga hold her tongue; it was getting late; it was drizzling that afternoon and taxis were hard to come by; yet she hated herself for not stopping the cab and getting out, hated herself for the ignoble (enforced, she felt) masquerade. She'd retorted with an uneasy mixture of pleading and defiance, "But the property is kept up so well—I mean,

they"—and "they" sat on her tongue like a toad—"they
. . . they all seem to be quite well off."

The driver, shooting a stinging glance into his mirror
as though he'd picked up a Communist or something
worse, muttered before falling into silence, "Well . . .
for my money, it's the end of the place. If you know
what I mean. *Them* in there. Like, they have places of
their own, don't they?"

When Olga got out in front of her large pampered
lawn, she threw the taxi fare onto the driver's seat,
depressed and frightened, angry with herself to the
point of crying. It was only a small assuagement, only
a half-satisfying irony when Finley, normally playing
golf on Saturday, popped out of the house into the
drizzling rain, giving full view of his deep chocolate
skin to the driver. "Hi, honey," he had said, "you're a
little late, aren't you? What did you buy?"

There it was again! Those were not leaves . . . those
were *not* leaves. Olga looked up to see whether Sophie
or Finley had heard it, her fingers manipulating the
needles even faster, as if by this domestic magic she
might ward off any peril, any disaster. Finley, as he had
been doing on and off since dinner, absently picked at
a short thread that bound the toe of his sock. He continued to read the paper, intently, as though not to miss
a paragraph. Sophie stopped playing the Mozart sona-

tina and began pacing back and forth in front of the bay window, but Olga could not tell whether Sophie had heard anything or had merely become impatient after flubbing for the third or fourth time the cadenza in the first movement. It was apparently the cadenza, for she settled again at the piano bench and in an exaggerated, slow tempo thumped out the descending triplets with fierce determination, pursing her lips.

Sophie. It disturbed Olga that her daughter clung to her childhood habit of pursing her lips into a pinched and prissy contour, but it was really more than disturbing: had Olga been a reflective woman, she would have realized her emotion was closer to anger; she would have perhaps admitted that the lip-pursing she'd not been able to tease, cajole, or punish Sophie into stopping was but another token of defeat in the unending battle in which she'd been engaged with her daughter. Rather than admit defeat, admit the anger of the defeat, Olga would say to friends and neighbors—archly, with a silvery rise to her voice—"It really disturbs me that Sophie is so plain."

Sophie, in fact, was not plain: her nose was very much like Olga's—straight, well-shaped, and proportioned gently on her oval face; long lashes shaded her light brown eyes (the color of Finley's), and the maple-syrup hue of her skin had not a flaw. It was true that Sophie's movements, her stance, were often boyish and coltish, but it was part of Olga's blindness to refuse to see that

these were defiance rather than permanent blights.
Whenever Olga reacted to Sophie's provocations, real
or imagined, she usually succeeded only in displaying
her own vulnerability; it was her misfortune that she
was all too often her own destroyer, her own executioner.
It was she who was most vulnerable when she said to
Sophie, a little too insistently, her voice pitched a little
too high, "Now stop that. Just stop it."

"Stop what?" Sophie asked, her hands poised over a
triplet of the cadenza.

Of course, Olga was not speaking of the determined
repetition of the cadenza, and Sophie seemed to sense
this; Olga was referring to Sophie's pacing back and
forth before the bay window. Logically, Olga should
have admonished Sophie then, and not many seconds
after the fact, but her hands had continued flying with
the needles in and out of the blue yarn, and the lie
she'd told herself—that the sound was only leaves, that
they were not footsteps—would not stick. She now no
longer trusted herself to silence.

"Stop what?" Sophie asked again.

"I saw you, for heaven's sake! Do you think I'm
blind?" The knitting beneath her fingers was fast be-
coming a disaster of gaping holes and shaggy ends. "All
that pacing up and down. Fidgeting. It's making me
nervous."

"Well, you ought to be nervous. You ought to be."
Sophie took off her round, steel-rimmed glasses and

rubbed her eyes. "I mean, Christ," she said, "what do you and Daddy pay taxes for? I mean, the police could —could've—"

"Could what, Sophie? Could what?"

"Oh, for crissake, Mother, every time I try to explain anything—oh, forget it." She turned, looked at the troublesome cadenza, and bit the white steel rim of her glasses. Then, quietly, looking toward the hall clock, she said, "I just can't stop thinking about those letters, though. Maybe they *are* crazy, just like you and Daddy said, but suppose they—"

"The letters, the letters," Olga said, her voice harsh above her clicking needles, "I told you they were crank letters. I've told you fifteen dozen times."

"That's what you say. . . ." Sophie played a measure of triplets absently, looking again at the clock. "You keep on saying that. . . ." Her fingers held on to a G-minor triad until its sound drifted away. "But you know, it really would have been just as easy for the police—"

"Crank letters, Sophie, crank letters! How many times do I have to tell you they're crank letters?" Olga ripped a needle out of a ragged row of stitches. "*Do* something, for pity's sake."

"Do what?" Sophie managed to make her voice both condescending and obsequious. She inspected imaginary smudges on her glasses.

"Anything, for pity's sake, I don't care. You're making me nervous." Olga began another row of knits and purls. "Make Daddy a drink. Or—or—if you can't think of anything to do, go upstairs and straighten out that messy closet of yours. I was looking in it the other day. Perfectly good sweaters all jumbled up just as if you thought money grew on—"

"Daddy, d'you want a drink?"

Finley, like many men who live in a household of women, had learned an art of gentle deception: he could murmur "hmm" in a number of intonations; the attack, inflection, the timbre, could be interpreted as yes, no, maybe, oh-you-don't-say, depending upon the expected or desired response. When his antennae were properly adjusted, he could by this device often handle lengthy and fairly intricate conversations with a minimum of actual engagement.

Since Sophie's question had been perfunctory and spiteful, she did not linger to divine whether his "hmm" meant no, yes, or maybe, but instead she pivoted on her faded blue sneakers and walked back and forth in front of the bay window, only to irritate Olga further. Her small clenched fists dug into the pockets of her blue denim skirt.

"Well, do *something*, Sophie. Don't drive me crazy with that—with that *stalking* about. I swear, you're the most unladylike young woman in all of St. Al—"

"Oh, Christ."

Olga stole a glance at the hall clock. "Oh, Christ what?"

"Just 'Oh, Christ' is all," Sophie said, slumping upon the piano bench and glaring at the Mozart as though she might tear it to shreds.

"Well, stop cursing."

"I wasn't cursing."

"No?" Olga noted that it was a quarter to ten. Her heart beat faster beneath the beige raw silk of her dress. "You were using the Lord's name in vain, which as you should know by now is just as bad."

"Whose Lord? Not mine." Sophie straddled the piano bench, planting her hands flatly on the dark mahogany. "I told you I don't believe in God."

Whether this was true or not, Olga didn't really know. Her daughter had made the announcement in her best Tarryfield voice, a sort of throaty drawl she'd picked up from her classmates at that expensive private school, and the remark, like the accent, might merely have been one of her latest affectations. In any case, Olga could not resist fighting back; she replied, disguising the pettiness of the squabble with parental disapproval, "It's gone to your head, hasn't it?" She pretended to count stitches so as to give moment and import to her thrust. "Hasn't it, this Bennington business, hmm?"

"Bennington? What's Bennington got to do with it?" Sophie pulled her glasses down to the tip of her nose, deliberately, it seemed to Olga, in an attempt to look plain.

"Oh? You think I haven't noticed, don't you?" The wool was very hot in her hands. It began to look uglier with each added stitch, but she continued, knitting faster and talking faster. "Hmm? All this—this practicing. Ever since your acceptance came, you've been—well, let's admit it, you've been practicing."

"*Prac*ticing? Practicing what, for crissake?"

"Hasn't she been practicing, Finley? Finley?" Olga leaned toward the coffee table and gave three little taps on the marble top with her needle. "Finley?"

"Um? What? What's that?" Finley barely lowered the paper. He glanced up, then turned the page. His toe was hooked into the top of his house slipper, and he dangled the slipper, as a pendulum, slowly.

"Practicing what, Mother?"

"You know as well as I."

"What?" Sophie, still straddling the piano bench, ran her fingers over several keys, producing a snippy chromatic scale. "If I knew, I wouldn't—"

"How to be . . ." Olga began and then trailed off into silence, listening again to the leaves in the wind.

"What, tell me what?"

"How to be modern and witty. And—and unkind."

"Oh, Mother."

"And don't 'oh, Mother' me. You know perfectly—"

Sophie interrupted Olga with a flagrantly discordant

thump upon the piano keys. Then she jumped up, yanked off her glasses, and said, "Oh, Christ, oh, Christ." She put her glasses back on and went over to the glass bowl sitting on the second ledge of the bookcase. The bowl was oblong. Cut-glass. Glittery as polished quartz. Inside it lay the letters.

"You're—you're," Olga said, faster than her needles dipped in and out of the yarn, "cursing again. It's the very last time I'm—"

"Oh, cursing . . . really, Mother . . ."

"You were. You were. You were using—"

"Using the Lord's name in vain," Sophie said, turning, ignoring for a minute the letters in the bowl. "And what's this God bit you keep fussing about all of a sudden? Every time I start to—to—I mean, you and Daddy never *saw* the inside of a church until four or five months ago."

Sophie left the bookcase, slouched past the liquor cabinet, and sat on the mustard cushions in the bay-window seat. As she mumbled derisions between the pinching of her lips, she traced with her sneaker the designs on the carved rug.

Olga heard the word "relevant," or thought she had, and heard what probably had been "moral responsibility" (for these were currently Sophie's favorite words, and they were, Olga felt, worked to death), but whatever else she'd said was lost in the shuffling of Finley's newspaper. Sophie was still tracing with her toe patterns on the rug when Olga heard her say something about St. Thomas Episcopal Church, the pithy codicil being "Just because they started letting a few blacks trickle in, you seem to think—"

"Negro, Sophie. How many times must I tell you?" Her voice went up, in a fluted ring. "Not black. Negro. It's tiresome enough your—your playing around with atheism and everything, but you needn't use that awful militant word as well."

She stopped pretending to knit. She placed the yarn and the needles on her lap. She longed for a confrontation, a battle, with anyone over anything, for it had become increasingly difficult to remain silent and wait for ten o'clock. Sophie had her hands clasped over her ears, as if to blot out anything else Olga might say; her elbows rested on her bare knees and she stared at the laces in her sneakers. She, too, was waiting for ten o'clock, Olga decided. Finley, who had again slipped his foot out of his house slipper, picked at the loose thread at his toe. Olga watched him, trying to decide if he were picking faster, more nervously, or whether she merely imagined it.

He, of course, had told her over and over that the letters were nonsense, that they were not blackmail letters as Sophie insisted, and that to give them credence would indicate a mental unbalance nearly as obvious as that of the sender. The letters, notes actually, had begun arriving in August. There were five altogether, each one typed on a coarse sheet of white paper. They were short, terse; the first four simply read: *Reparations by September 8. The Committee.* The last letter said: *Reparations by ten o'clock. YU 2-4357.*

Olga looked around her living room and tried to forget about the time. She was pleased with the arrangement of the room, her choice of pieces, her things. Although she was not aware of it (visitors, however, often were), she'd decorated the room just as she dressed herself, in complementary colors—off-white walls, a pale gold carved rug, beige silk for the sofa and armchairs. It was not entirely vanity that caused Olga Blake to dress her house as she dressed herself and to attach inordinate pride to her furnishings—even if she did demand of Lucille, the day maid, in addition to her regular chores, that she rub lemon polish twice a week into the dark wood of the spinet, that she rub to a high shine the brown porcelain horses at the hearth, that the books and china pieces be removed twice weekly for a thorough dusting.

It was not altogether vanity; it was partly that Olga considered her furnishings her credentials, her passport into a world of opulence she'd never before known; it was as if all her material goods (including a second car, a station wagon she'd still not learned to drive) were assurances that those mean days of her Southern childhood and those mean days on West 117th Street, when every penny mattered, were over, would never return.

Her furnishings (including the silverware about which
Sophie'd once maliciously said, "Mother, if Lucille
polishes those things one more time, she's going to rub
them clear out of existence") were less items to be
presently used and enjoyed than they were amulets to
ward off the memory of a bitter past.

The teddy bear was another matter. It had nearly
always been in the Blake household. A huge stuffed
animal, three feet three inches tall, which always sat
like a third presence in the room, had been bought for
Sophie when she was four or five; it had not been
bought at F. A. O. Schwarz for adult amusement, as a
conversation piece, although ironically it was the bear
that guests most frequently talked about, remembered
—not the large sofa of raw silk, or the redwood liquor
cabinet, or the glittering brown horses at the hearth.
The teddy bear, with his pink glass eyes, now sat in his
armchair as if listening to the wind.

Olga did not dare rise and go place the blue knitted
wool across the bear's chest, to try it, to pretend to see
if the sweater size were correct, for both Finley and
Sophie would notice at a glance the scraggly knitting
with its sloppy holes and see it had been badly botched.
She stopped listening to the shuffling of leaves outside
on the garden stones and looked at Sophie, who'd dug
the letters out of the glass bowl and now stood in front
of Finley and his newspaper, gesticulating, shouting,
really, shaking the dog-eared letters at her father. "But

how *can* you, Daddy?" Sophie spoke with such vehe-
mence that it seemed the subject was entirely new and
had not been batted about for weeks. "How can you,"
she cried, her round glasses slipping down to the end of
her nose, "just—just *sit* there and dismiss these—this
whole business?"

Finley smoothed out the wrinkles in the paper across
his worsted trousers. He started his usual placation with
"Oh, now, Sophie, come on," but she seemed determined
not to accept it.

"I mean," she interrupted, looking quickly at the
clock by the staircase, "just suppose all this junk isn't
just a sick—sick sort of—I mean, what if they *aren't*
crank letters, Daddy, that's what I mean."

Olga's voice burst into the room, so choked that Sophie
and Finley turned sharply. "Crank!" she said. "Crank
letters, that's all." Tears, which seemed more in her
throat than in her eyes, blocked her voice, strangled her
words. "I told you, I've told you, and you won't believe
me. Damn you, Sophie," she whispered and threw down
upon the coffee table the blue wool entwined with
its silver needles. "Sophie . . . Sophie," she mouthed
rather than spoke, just before the telephone rang.

The shrilling intrusion sounded like a siren of disaster, and Finley's taut attentiveness to the piercing rings,
his delay in answering, frightened her nearly as much
as the sound of the phone itself. Did he, even during
the past weeks of proclaiming the letters to be nonsense

and belittling her uneasiness, really, deep down, believe there might be something to them after all? Frozen on the sofa, she waited for him to answer. It was seven minutes to ten. She waited for him to answer.

"Hello," Finley said, his voice unfriendly. "Yeah, who's speaking? What? Oh, Scotty! For God's sake, didn't recognize you. So, what's up?"

It was Scotty, Scotty Sykes, only a neighbor, but that consolation was, as Olga glanced at the clock, a small one. She pressed a Kleenex to the dampness in the wrinkles around her neck. Normally these wrinkles could distract her from nearly any unpleasantness— taxes, social snubs, headaches—for she knew her figure remained trim, her legs shapely, her face attractive. She could never quite forgive fate for allowing wrinkles to appear at her neck so early in life and so undeniably; if weight had been a problem, she would have gladly starved; if her nose had not been to her liking, she would have had it fixed; but no amount of cosmetic tinkering could successfully hide the ravishments of time about her neck. Having been blessed physically in so many other ways, she could normally, basking in resentment and self-pity, count upon her wrinkles for dependable, if bitter, distraction.

Finley hung up the phone and went back to his chair near the Bloomingdale lamp. He picked up his paper. "It was Scotty. Scotty down the street."

"What in the world does he want at this hour? Is Sybil all right?"

"Sybil? I suppose so. Why?"

"Gallstones, I'm told," Olga said, not unaware that she herself had never been sick—except for an April, an April long ago, and that had been something far worse than mere sickness. "Or did she tell me kidney stones?" Finley made no comment. "Anyway, she's got stones." Finley was again deep into his newspaper. Raising her voice, preparing for an argument, she cried, "Well, if it wasn't Sybil, what's he want?"

"A power mower," Finley mumbled. "He's finally got that power mower—you know, that he's been talking about all summer. You know, for the yard. Wanted me to see it."

Olga, without her knitting, felt lost, yet she could not pick it up again. It was ugly. Besides, her hands were damp and they were shaking. She wanted to bash Finley's newspaper fortress away from his face, but instead she said, "Scotty Sykes. I swear, he's like some kid with a choochoo."

Finley dangled his slipper on the end of his big toe.

"A power mower, indeed!" She was rewarded only with the soft tap of the dangling slipper on his stockinged heel.

With her voice rising, highly peppered with incredulity, she said, "And in the middle of the night?"

"Come on, Olga," Finley said, lowering his paper, "it's not even ten yet. Sometimes I think your daughter *is* right. Huh, Sophie?" He dropped his paper and winked at Sophie, who was not very responsive to his jocularity. "What's that you're always accusing your mother of? Hyper-something or other?" He walked toward the liquor cabinet. "Brandy all gone?"

"Hyperbolic," Sophie said, pacing up and down behind the sofa in the direction of the study and the kitchen with her fists in the pockets of her denim skirt. "Mother does," she said vaguely, looking at the clock, "have tendencies towards being hyper—"

"Oh, Finley, for heaven's sake, it's staring you straight in the face. Right next to the gin." Then quickly, fearing another bout of silence, Olga said, "And even if it's not exactly the middle of the night, it's too late to be hightailing it down the street just to look at somebody's silly—"

"I *said* I wasn't going, Olga. Now cut it out."

"Well, *go* if you want to. Don't let me stop you. Go."

"Look, I told Scotty I'd come by tomorrow. So what's all the fuss?"

"Fuss? There's no fuss, my dear, who's fussing? I just meant you might as well be down the street at Scotty's as here. I mean, your head's been stuck in that lurid paper since—ever since dinner and you've—"

"Lurid? *The Wall Street Journal?*"

"Well, your head's been stuck in it. You might as well be at Scotty's—or somewhere off in space as far as—"

"All right, Olga, damn it, all right. I *will* go. Jesus. Yap, yap, yap. It'll be a relief just not to—"

"No, Daddy! Please . . . I . . . okay, I'm silly, but please don't go. Those—those," Sophie said, pointing to the letters in the bowl, "they said ten o'clock. The last one said by—"

"We're back at those crank letters again, are we?" Olga plumped a sofa cushion and blinked smartly at Sophie. "*Now* who's being hyperbolic? Hmm?"

But she really was not interested in baiting Sophie, in instigating another fight, and she turned and buried her face in the palm of her right hand. Her hair fell forward, covering the sides of her face, and the nails of her middle finger and her forefinger poked through the strands of her hair as if they were horn growths. Her left hand caressed her right elbow in her lap and then fell to her slender knees. The grace and narcissism of this gesture seemed to help her speak, but it did not ease the hard monotone of her words. "Nobody," she said, speaking into her palm, into her wrist, "can blackmail anybody if there's nothing to blackmail anybody for, now can they? Now, can they? Finley, have you done anything to be blackmailed for?"

Olga did not look up, nor did she expect an answer; she had for many weeks gone through the same questions and answers as though it were a necessary ritual, a liturgy. "You, Sophie? Of course not. We're as respectable as anybody in St. Albans. Even more so. Are we not?"

She took her hand away from her face, as if to get air, as if she'd been at the point of suffocation, and in a breathless pinched voice, she said, as much to the objects and furnishings of her room as to Sophie and Finley, *"Aren't we?"*

With an inward wail, which neither Sophie nor Finley could hear but knew to be there only from the working of her trembling mouth, she grabbed a sofa pillow, and rocking gently with it, pressed it tightly to her breast. " 'The number,' " Olga said, weaving back and forth slowly upon the sofa, her eyes blank, " 'you have dialed is not in service at this time. This is a recording. The number you have—' "

"What?" Finley sat down next to Olga. Sophie sat at Olga's other side.

Finley stopped Olga's weaving and gently shook her shoulder. "What, Olga? What did you say?"

" 'The number you have dialed is . . . is . . .' " The salt of her tears burned a small chafed spot on her lower lip, and when Finley pressed his brandy glass to her mouth, the spot burned even more, but she continued, looking down into the small pool of amber brandy Finley held before her, "Yes, yes, oh yes, I did call. I did call. I called the number on that letter, Finley, I did. I couldn't stand not knowing. I just couldn't stand it. But . . . but . . . Finley?" She looked up from the brandy glass. "What's it got to do with us? Who is the Committee, who really is the Committee, Finley? It is a mistake, isn't it? Isn't it? They really are, aren't they, crank letters, aren't they? Even the police think they—"

"The police? Olga?"

Her fingers, like frenzied sparrows, threatened to take flight. She put them between her knees to stop their shaking. " 'The—the number,' " she began again, tears falling on her dress, into the brandy, " 'you have dialed is not in—' "

"Olga! Now, stop, Olga. Darling, now stop. What—now what about the police? You said the police what?"

"The police. Yes. Yes, I did. I mean, it was the logical thing, wasn't it? But they said, like you said, they said they were crank letters. Save them. Call them. Call them if—if—I mean, they were nice and everything, but they said they were likely only crank letters, but I—the letters were—I mean, when those awful letters kept coming and you kept telling me to chuck them out and I kept hearing all sorts of things in the yard when you were late getting back and Sophie was out and the rose bushes seemed to—to *move* in the night, even with no breeze at all, and the birds down by the barbecue pit, Finley, kept on with all that racket and—I—I . . ."

Olga could not continue and her tears had transformed Finley and the glass of brandy into a blur. She picked up her knitting and had meant to wipe her face with it, but instead she cried into it, and with hoarse chokes said what she'd forced back all evening: "I'm afraid, I'm afraid, oh God, I'm afraid."

Before Finley could put down his glass, with one arm she pulled his head onto her bosom and with her other arm she pulled Sophie to her neck, the knitting quivering before her in her trembling hands. She rocked back and forth on the seat of the sofa, holding fast to Finley and Sophie, rocking them, too, as though they were children, as though they were children in need of their lullabies. The silver needles slid out of the wool and clinked upon the tabletop, but she clung to the yarn, pressing it to her opened mouth, and she clung to her husband and daughter, rocking them, as if it were they who needed care, needed attention, and perhaps, too, as if they were objects, like her porcelain horses and pale gold rug, that she feared she might soon have to part with.

Finley's drink had spilled to the floor, staining the rug brown. Sophie's legs were awkwardly placed, threatening to tilt the coffee table. Olga noticed both things simultaneously, and it sobered her quickly, but she had not understood, as she released them, that it had taken a moment of hysteria to make her display overtly any sign of affection; somewhere over the years of survival and striving upward, her love for Finley had become prosaic and perfunctory, and with Sophie it was possible that love did not exist. Her instinct was to continue to cling, to find solace for her fear in their communion. But she did not realize that love is the very last emotion that may be taken for granted; it cannot flower without attention and nourishment. Out of habit, and out of the discomfort of indulging in unpracticed sentiments, each

—Sophie, Finley, Olga—hastily retreated behind his armor.

Sophie now said, "I'm sorry. I'm sorry, Mother. You acted—"

"That's all right," Olga told her.

"But I really am sorry, Mother. Really."

"That's all right."

"But you never *said* anything about—about going to the police or anything. I mean, all along you were acting just like those letters were bills from Lord & Tay—"

"I said it was all right, Sophie! For pity's sake, I said it was all right."

"Okay now," Finley said, "stop it, you two. Just calm down. Nobody," he said, gathering up his newspaper again, "is about to bother a middle-aged gynecologist in the middle of the night in the middle of St. Albans."

He shook the paper as though he were airing it out, as though the soft rustle were a coda to the anxiety that had beset the room. Yet, after a few seconds of silence, he lowered the paper and peered over at Olga and Sophie sitting on the sofa, saying as an afterthought, "Reparations—bah! It's got to be a mistake—or a joke. They think we're Nazis or something?"

Neither replied and he again lifted his paper, blocking off his chocolate, placid face, the receding black-silver wiry twists of his hair. The silence, however, seemed to accuse, for he lowered the paper once more and said, "It's only some nasty joke, okay?" When neither of them responded to his comfortless balm, he said, "Well, turn on the television or—or—Sophie, why don't you play? Come on, come on. Relax."

Olga studied the stain on the rug and, without looking up, she said to Sophie, "Yes, Sophie, why don't you, dear? Johnny Carson doesn't come on until 11:30, and it's—it's—"

"Damn it, Olga," Finley said, throwing his paper to the floor, "it's two minutes past ten! Two minutes *past.* You satisfied? That—that so-called Committee hasn't phoned. And they won't." He picked up the paper, blowing out exasperated breath into the room in general. "Now will you settle down? *Please?*"

Olga fluffed the sofa cushions, avoiding a glance at the clock by the stairs. "I *am* settled down. Almost. Mozart, Sophie," she said, fishing for a magazine in the rack at her side. "Play that nice quiet Mozart piece. You know," she said, unable to resist illustrating with a quick gesture in the air Sophie's Mozartian fingers. Then she jerked her fingers back to her lap, suddenly ashamed of herself. "That piece with the little trickle that goes up and down in the right hand."

Sophie did not miss the parody, and said with a lofty detachment, "Most all of Mozart has a little trickle that goes up and down in the right hand."

"Sophie!" Finley said from behind his paper. "Enough

of that tartness, now." He looked around the edge of the paper mildly and added, "Be decent to your mother for a change."

"Yes, at least you might try once in a while to—" but Sophie drowned out Olga's words with the Mozart, complying with fake enthusiasm to her parents' request. Before her sarcastic fingers got very far into the andante movement, the telephone rang.

It rang for a long time before Finley answered it. Olga stood. Sophie's fingers, like brown marble, lay on the piano keys.

"Hello! Oh . . . yes, yes. Wait a second." Finley turned to Olga and said, "It's Scotty again. He and Sybil want to know if we can do bridge with them tomorrow. Round about nine."

For the second time that night Olga felt she'd been led to the brink of some abyss, to the edge of a dangerous precipice, only to find jolly old Scotty standing below in a safe shallow shoal. Hardly realizing it, she walked to the fireplace and stood shaking, trembling. Her hands fluttered over objects—glass cats, tin owls, snuffboxes— and she said with barely suppressed hysteria, "Yes! O God, tell them yes!" and smashed to the hearth, into tiny pieces, something she'd had in her hands. It had been a figurine, a giraffe of fragile glass, but it had been necessary to smash it; it had been necessary to *do* something. Yet even afterward, as Finley talked on and on to Scotty, making some sort of arrangement about bringing the power mower over, her fingers would not stop fluttering; she had to clench them in order to stave off further destruction at the mantel or about the living room.

Finley had scarcely put down the phone when it rang again—or at first she thought it had. It was not the phone. It was not the telephone.

The doorbell rang. Not very urgently. It was a civilized ring. Finley answered it. The door was hardly ajar when, as if by a strong wind, it swept inward, knocking Finley off balance, back toward the end of the stairwell. In the blowing September night, framed by the door, stood a man and a woman. Olga had never seen Afro hairdos quite that violent before. The young man, very tall and very black, wore a dashiki and khaki trousers. The long-legged woman with him could not possibly have had on a brassière. They both wore tiny gold earrings pierced in their left ears. It was not until the man, smiling through exceedingly uniform teeth, said, "Greetings," that Olga noticed the cold gleam of the switchblade in his large black hand.

(2)

"**OKAY, SIT,**" the tall man said. He tapped the flat side of his knife against Finley's neck. "All y'awl sit," he said, kicking the front door shut with the heel of his ankle boot. "Check around, Hedda. Ain't s'pose to be nobody here, but take a look."

The woman with long-legged speed glided past Olga and looked into the rooms leading off from the living room—the study, the dining area, the kitchen. She had a sharp, thin-boned chin above her long neck, and the lids of her eyes were half-lowered as if she seldom found anything worth her full attention. About her lips there was a suggestion of a sneer that, either out of restraint or boredom, did not come into bloom. She was older than Sophie by perhaps ten years; she was probably twenty-eight or thirty, about the same age as the tall man with the knife.

"You," Olga said to the man, "you're—you're the Committee?"

"I do the asking, baby, just sit and shut up." He scraped at the underside of a button on Finley's shirt as though he intended to pry it off. "You Blake?"

Finley, who was trying to regain some portion of his dignity as well as to rise from the foyer floor, said, "Now look here. . . ." He got up but did not seem to know how to continue. "If—if you think—"

"Blake?"

"Finley Blake," Finley said, his hands extended outward in supplication. "And—and put away that knife. I mean, there's no need for violence or—or . . . in point of fact, in point of fact, whatever cash, or whatever . . . I mean, there's nothing here much to rob. In fact, there's—"

"Man, are you for real?" the intruder said with a smile as cold as the gleam of the blade of his knife. "You think we want your jiveass TV or your fucking silverware?" He seemed to take pleasure in answering himself as he said, "Shee-ut!" Then he called out to the woman with him, "Hedda? Hedda?"

Hedda came back into the living room, her long legs in pink-tinted hose preceding her, leading the way: the woman's shoulders and neck seemed to follow her legs by a delayed second or two, giving her the disjointed movement of an animal scouting for prey. The sneer that never quite broke across her face bothered Olga almost as much as the man's knife.

"Nobody round, huh?" the man asked Hedda, shoving Finley toward a chair with the steel end of his knife. "What're them rooms for?" he asked, nodding in the direction from which she'd just come.

"How the fuck am I suppose to know?" Her voice sounded as Olga expected it to—husky, assured, and, though the words were vulgar, the sound was not unpleasant. "Rooms. Dinette. Kitchen. A den or something." Like talons, her hands rested on her thin hips, hips covered with a dress the color of tomato consommé. "Ain't nobody else here, Fargo. The Committee knows enough not to send—"

"Look, Hedda. Look anyway. Check upstairs."

The man relaxed a bit when Finley sat down. He now held the knife loosely at his side. "See what that light's doing on—the one we saw upstairs on the front side. Take a look."

"Oh, holy shit, Fargo," Hedda said, objecting but nevertheless moving to go upstairs, "after twenty minutes of casing this place, we would've—"

"Hed-da," Fargo said, breaking her name into impatient syllables.

Then he spotted the teddy bear. He stared at it. His black satin jaw went slack. He frowned. Sophie at this moment eased off the piano bench and ran toward the foyer, toward the front door, but her hand had barely touched the glass knob when Hedda, in a cat-leap back down the stairs, grabbed her by the hair, held her a second as if she might slap her about the face. Then she dropped her to the polished floor, like a dust rag.

"All right!" Finley jumped up. "All right, goddamn it, cut it out!" As he reached down to pick Sophie up, he said, "Just take what you want and get the hell out of here. What—"

Fargo, in three long strides, reached Finley and with his left hand in a loose fist struck him about the jaw and ears, knocking him to the floor beside Sophie. From a slanted opening in his dashiki Fargo pulled out a blue-black .22-caliber. He stood there, towering over Finley and Sophie, his face impassive except for a slight quiver of his eyebrow. "Man, you want some of this hot lead?" he asked, massaging the revolver's handle with his thumb. "Or some of this cold steel?" he added, pretending the alternatives were a joke, although he spoke without much levity. "Now get up there. Both of you. On that there couch." He pointed to the sofa where Olga, barely breathing, sat. "Next to her. There ain't no escaping, understand? There ain't no escaping. Okay, Hedda."

As Hedda went upstairs, Fargo replaced the revolver beneath the brown-green pattern of his dashiki and stood behind the sofa. "So at last," he said, "we've got Daddy Blake and Mama Blake and Baby Blake. Right?"

"What," Olga asked, modulating her tone so as not to offend but unable to still its imperious inflection, "do you want of us? What can you possibly want? I don't have much jewelry. Finley doesn't—"

"Shut up." He walked around to the front of the sofa and flicked, with a black button, the sharp blade in and out of its pearl incasement, shifting his eyes from Olga to Finley to Sophie. Suddenly, during his inspection, his eyes lit upon Olga's brooch, a small cluster of brilliants and sapphires pinned to the beige silk of her dress. He looked at it and smiled, and then as the smile left his face, he snatched it off, tearing her dress as he pulled it.

"Your fucking jewelry—shee-ut!"

He dropped the brooch into Olga's lap and then shifted his gaze to the left, past Sophie, to the teddy bear sitting in his stuffed chair with the crocheted doilies. He went over to the bear and pulled it to its feet. "Ain't *this* a motherfucker!"

"Nobody's up there, Fargo," Hedda said as she came down the stairs. "I told you it wasn't nobody up— what's that thing?"

"A goddamn giant teddy bear," Fargo said, poking his knuckles into the animal's stomach. "Are you ready for this? Man, I've seen some way-out things in my day, but this is a sonofabitch." A smile broke out beneath his high cheekbones; it looked like a pearly pool in a black landscape. "Dig this thing, Hedda. Are you ready for this?"

"Holy shit," she said, poking the bear's pink eyes, as if trying to blind it. "Whose is it?"

Fear rather than meanness prompted Olga to say, "Well, tell her, Sophie, for God's sake, tell her." The admonitory ring in Olga's voice, particularly since Sophie had not had time to reply, riveted the inquisitors' attention: they looked at Olga, studied her, as if the teddy bear no longer mattered. Olga was unable to retreat. They looked at *her* instead of Sophie, instead of the bear. "Well, tell them. It is yours, isn't it? Isn't it?"

"Mother."

"Well? Well? I mean, I didn't have to keep it around cluttering up the place, you know, and—and—" They looked at her, the lynx-eyed woman and the handsome man. "Well, answer me, Sophie," she said, feeling as though she'd been backed into a corner.

Sophie, pinching her mouth, glared at Olga.

"*Answer* me," Olga said. But Sophie held her tongue. "*Answer* me," she demanded.

"Oh, hush up, bitch," Hedda finally snapped, dropping the bear to the floor, suddenly losing interest. Although the lids over her large hazel eyes were half-closed, giving her a careless, languid appearance, she spoke curtly. "If there's one thing we don't need it's a hysterical cunt screaming all over the—"

"*Don't* call me a—a—" Olga could not bring herself to repeat the word. "How dare you! You—you—"

"Hedda Brewster, baby," Hedda said, sticking a stockinged leg forward and raising her chin. "But Miss Brewster to you, bitch."

Olga had been right; this was her enemy, her first enemy—far more than Fargo with his gun and his knife. Beneath the woman's sullen beauty and grace, Olga knew there beat a heart of concrete; she would be capable of doing anything; she had, this young woman, a taste for blood.

They seemed to be together, Hedda and Fargo—that is, there was something between them beyond a burglar team, something beyond a criminal alliance. Olga was not sure, but Hedda's sidewise glances toward Fargo, and her reluctant subservience, suggested that this might be so. It was this suspicion that made Olga direct her attention to Fargo, her words to Fargo; she flirted very cautiously, and almost (though not quite) imperceptibly, she stole glances at Hedda in a surreptitious appraisal of the pain it might cause her.

"If this is extortion, or—or—blackmail," Olga said, fingering her brooch, looking at Fargo, "it's ridiculous, it's absolutely ridiculous."

She watched him manhandling her tin owls and her Venetian glass on the mantel. "Don't think for one minute you'll get away with it. Not for a minute. Do you understand that?" Her attention was directed entirely toward Fargo and her "you," she made very clear, was singular. She was pleased that she'd managed to exclude the sullen young woman.

"I've told the police," she went on, which was really not a lie, but realizing at the same time how right Sophie had been, how silly she and Finley had been in sidestepping the whole matter by attempting to sweep it under the carpet. "And all the neighbors," she added, which was a lie, for she'd not even mentioned the letters to Scotty or Sybil.

"Oh, yes, yes," Olga repeated, "I've told them. I've told them. And there's no money here—I mean, less than a hundred or so—and silverware and the television set and—and what I mean," she said, her voice halting, losing its authority as Hedda took one of Finley's ciga- rettes from the coffee table, lit it, and blew a stream of blue smoke down over the sofa into her face, "is—is what I mean is, for God's sake, if you're being robbers and brutal and forcing yourselves into people's houses, why don't you just be professional about it? Why don't—"

"Olga," Finley said.

"No, no, Finley," she went on quickly while she still had steam, "there's no point in being intimidated by that gun and that knife and this—all this slummy talk. Logically, they simply should take whatever—"

"Olga!" Finley said again.

Sophie waved Hedda's smoke from her face. "It's best. Don't, Mother."

"Man!" said Fargo, walking over toward the liquor cabinet. "Look at this cat's stash! Chivas Regal. Johnnie Walker. Beefeater. Hey—wanna taste, Hedda?"

Kicking the teddy bear over on his belly, she said, "Why the fuck not—we might as well do something till they call."

" 'They' are calling?" Olga asked. *"They* are? You aren't the Committee, then?" She turned from Hedda to Fargo. Neither answered.

Even after Hedda brought ice cubes in from the kitchen and she and Fargo sat nursing unbelievably large helpings of scotch, there was little information to be gathered from them. It was as if they were, in some private game of toying and tormenting, withholding the reasons for their being there, as if it gave them sadistic pleasure and unaccustomed power to be in charge of the living room with its confused and frightened owners. It seemed to Olga that they were not professionals at whatever their evil business was, but having no experience with crime, she could not say for sure that they were amateurs, merely thugs. In either case, she and Finley and Sophie were faced with danger and their distress was real.

Fargo left his perch on the arm of the chair usually occupied by Finley, and with his drink he went over to the spinet. "Who plays this here piano?" he asked.

Sophie took her time answering. Finally, she said, "I do."

"Yeah?" He sat down on the bench with his drink and with a blurry pedal and misplaced notes began pounding his way through *Chopsticks.* After several stops and starts he said, "Come play me something. Come on over."

Sophie studied her blunted fingernails fondly. "No—I—don't know anything anymore. I'm—I'm really quite rusty."

Chopsticks turned into a heavy bang of his black fist on a cluster of white keys. "Don't hand me that shit!" Some of the alcohol, the Chivas Regal, splashed across his khaki trousers. He sat there, and then in a quieter voice, looking about the room as though he'd just entered it, said, "Come on—all right?"

For a few seconds he seemed almost congenial—Sophie's date for the evening, a guest asking for music—but this image did not last very long, for he said with measured meanness, "Look, baby, if you play, you play —if you don't play, you don't play."

His eyes shifted from Sophie to Olga and then to Finley. "Jesus, you goddamn bushwa niggers in your bushwa house with your bushwa piano. Man, what a bag you're in." And then to Sophie, with his thin lips puckered in an imitation, " 'I'm really quite rusty.' Shee-ut!"

"No one asked you to come to this—this—and the word you're trying to use is—is *bourgeois*," Sophie said, correcting him with icy tranquillity. "I mean," she continued with obvious logic, "you can leave if we're so disgusting. Nobody *asked* you to come. Nobody—"

"The Committee did, baby, the Committee did, and don't you forget it." Fargo set his drink on top of the piano and took out his knife. The blade began a nervous hide-and-seek in and out of its case. "And if I say bushwa, that's the way it is."

He pushed back the piano bench and stood up, exposing and hiding the nervous blade, exposing and hiding it, as if in some demonstration of an obscenity. "You say it the way *you* say it, and I say it the way *I* say it. Dig?" He sat down at the piano and began, with careless thrusts, to jab the knife blade into the spaces between the white keys in the bass clef.

"Don't, for crissake!" Sophie jumped up from the sofa to stop him.

"Sophie!" Finley shouted, half standing.

Sophie ignored Finley and, although she did not dare try to take the knife from Fargo, she did hold fast to his arm. "You goon! You'll ruin it! You'll ruin it!"

Fargo smiled. He clamped his fingers about her wrist. With a soft muffled thud, the blade sucked back into its shelter. "Play me some piano," he said, looking at Sophie, trapped in his grip, his head tilted to the side.

"Let go of me."

"Come. Play me some piano."

"Let her alone, you bully," Olga said, rising from the sofa along with Finley.

Fargo, still clamping tightly to Sophie's wrist, said to Olga, with a slow show of teeth, "Sit down. Let's don't start nothin' now."

"Fargo, you a bastard," Hedda said, with assumed

indifference, but the rasp in her voice belied the pretense. "Stop molesting that child."

"Hell, I ain't molesting the chick. . . . She's gonna play me some piano." Fargo waited, staring down into Sophie's face. "Aren't you, baby? Aren't you?" He pressed Sophie's rebellious shoulder and pulled her nearer to him, closer to him. "You gonna play me some piano, huh?"

Sophie, quiescent, pursing her mouth into its tight frown, said, "Let go of me."

"I said play the fucking piano."

Finley stood up again. "Now, see here. There's no point in—"

"I don't want no shit from you, man. Dig? Now, sit back down."

Hedda's fingers nipped into Finley's shoulder with a hint of karate knowledge. He sat down. "Relax, buster," she said. "Get a drink and get your nerves together."

"Gonna play?" Fargo asked again, smiling down into Sophie's face, his hand holding her rigid body a second away from his lean frame.

"For crissake, why?"

"I like the piano, baby." Fargo's nose came closer to Sophie's face. He'd stopped smiling. "I want you to play me some piano."

"Christ, you wouldn't understand it if I did."

"Why wouldn't I?"

"You wouldn't."

"Try me."

"Let go."

"You won't play me some piano?"

"No, you bastard, no!"

"Name's Fargo, Sophie. Name's Fargo." His face was quiet black satin. He pressed into her body. "I'd like some nice piano, Sophie. I dig some nice piano. I—" His lips came closer to Sophie's face and stopped firmly over her mouth as she squirmed and beat him on the chest with one free hand and kicked at his glossy ankle boots.

Finley had already grasped the metal ashtray on the coffee table and had it aimed in the direction of Fargo's head as Hedda intercepted with one light chop of her open hand across Finley's neck at the top of his spine. Her quick jab sent the ashtray rolling across the rug and forced Finley back again onto the sofa beside Olga. Sophie, whose mouth was trapped beneath Fargo's, no longer pummeled and sought to free herself; she now stood quietly pressed into Fargo's dashiki, her hands limply hanging at her sides.

Then, abruptly, with a rude release, Fargo let her go. Except for his jerky breathing, he appeared thoroughly uninterested in what he'd done. Sophie, too, seemed untouched by the enforced embrace, and as she walked away from him, slowly, toward the liquor cabinet, she looked serene. She poured out an inch of sherry, and then, holding back her head, gargling with it, paused, and returned to face Fargo, who had not moved. The ritual ended as she spewed, spat out a spray of reddish-amber sherry into Fargo's face and across the top of his dashiki.

Hedda watched it all, her eyes tracing the proceedings as though she were not seeing right. "What?" She kicked at the ashtray near her foot. "What? Why, you little shit! Who the fuck you think you are?" She looked at the sherry running down Fargo's high black cheek. "Fargo, you let that—Fargo, you let that little bitch spit on you? Fargo? Fargo!"

Fargo's refusal to respond, his refusal to wipe away the sherry from his face, seemed to upset Hedda more than the insult itself. Her lip quivered and she stared at Fargo as if she intended by the force of her eyes to dispel his vacant trancelike gaze. Her eyes, now wide open, caught flicks of light from the lamp, transforming the sullen hazel into a glittery yellow. Olga did not doubt that it had been Hedda who had been most insulted, for Fargo gave the impression of taking his just deserts, or indeed as though in some perverse manner he had actually enjoyed the spewing punishment. Whatever Hedda felt, Olga could not immediately decide, but it was obvious that Hedda was in urgent need of retaliation. When her lip stopped its quivering, and when she saw that she was unsuccessful in goading Fargo into response, she turned on Sophie, who sat in Finley's chair wiping her mouth on a cocktail napkin.

"You," she said, her lip exposing a row of irregular teeth, "why, you dirty little—"

"No!" Olga shouted as Hedda started toward Sophie, "Don't touch her!" And then, with a cutting thrust—although she regretted it before it was out of her mouth—Olga said, "After all, it was entirely *their* affair."

One long leg was for a second suspended in midair as Hedda pivoted on the other to turn from Sophie to Olga. She grabbed a handful of hair and yanked Olga's head back. On the sofa, beneath the lamplight, Olga's skin looked whiter than ever. The wrinkles about her neck were exposed. Her dress was torn above the left breast where Fargo had snatched off her brooch. Hedda did not hit her, but merely held her head back with strong fingers entwined in her hair; it seemed as if Olga were being inspected, appraised. She sat there, trapped, X-rayed, and vulnerable to Hedda's gaze. But Hedda did not raise her hand, nor did she speak—at least not with words. There was, though, a promise: with half-lowered lids, the glare down upon Olga's face was burning; in good time, and with accuracy, Hedda would have her revenge.

As she loosened her fingers from Olga's hair, she said, "Well, it won't be long, sister, it won't be long. The Committee will take care of business." In a swooping,

gliding movement, she scooped from the coffee table
a pack of Finley's cigarettes, and digging one out with
her long nails she said, "You uptight, half-white, piss-
elegant motherfucker."

"All right, Hedda." Fargo had come out of his trance
and was at the cabinet putting ice cubes into his scotch.
"Cool it, man, cool it."

"Cool it, hell," she said, blowing a long burrowing
path of smoke across the top of the lampshade. "She's
lucky I don't smack the shit out of her."

Before Fargo could make any answer, Finley said,
"Say—uh—look, Fargo," his voice calm, clinical, "Let
me stand up a minute. All right?" He stood, put his
hands in his pockets, and began walking back and forth
in front of the coffee table before Fargo could grant or
deny his request. "Now, look here. We need—need to
come to some terms. For instance, look, let's put it this
way—"

"Straight, baby," Fargo said. "You got the floor."

"Obviously," Finley began, clearing his voice, watching his slippers as he walked over the rug, "you're—
you're quite well armed and I—I'm not a violent man,
as you must imagine, and well, I'm hardly going to
jeopardize my family by trying to disarm you—I mean,
you know, even if I could. I mean—"

"Get to the point, baby."

"Right," Finley said absently, scratching his silver-black hair. He continued to walk up and down before the coffee table for a bit and then said, "When Hedda mentioned just now—"

"Miss Brewster, baby," Hedda said, tapping her cigarette ashes on the rug, "and don't forget it."

"Miss Brewster," Finley said, touching an imaginary hat. "Your Committee. When she mentioned your Committee—well, is it, huh, like that thing we read about over in Jersey? You know, the Black Circle? Those militants, or that group—or whatever they were supposed to be—who—"

"Fascists, Finley," Olga said. "Black Fascists. Every single one of them."

"Quiet, Olga." Finley changed his pacing route, for Hedda was now seated on the coffee table, her long legs crossed, and she began to jiggle one leg outward in his path. "You know, Fargo, the group that went around in East Orange or somewhere in Jersey, and you know, went around terrorizing. Extorting. You know, getting funds from Negro professionals who—"

"Negro professionals, ha." Hedda's foot rubbed ashes into the rug. "You mean bushwa niggers out there with two cars, and two of this, and two of that, and trips to St. Thomas, with their Omega Omega this, and their Delta-Beta-up-my-ass? Is that what you mean?"

"I mean," Finley said, looking at his watch and stealing a glance at the clock near the staircase, "what I

mean is—what about your Committee? Are you con-
nected with that group in Jersey?"

Fargo, glass in hand, had his face close to the pane
of the bay window. "No connection, baby," he said,
fishing for the cord to close the mustard draperies. "The
Committee is organized, dig? It ain't no bullshittin'
operation like them cats over in Jersey." When he left
the window and approached the mirror above the mantel, he paused, quickly turning his head left and right
to steal a look at himself.

"You care if I get a drink?" Finley asked.

"It's your booze, man—go ahead."

As Finley poured out a whiskey, he said, "So it's—
it's the same sort of thing, really, isn't it? I mean, you're
sort of the same thing, I take it, huh?"

Fargo leaned on the mantel, placing a booted foot
on the back of a brown porcelain horse. "You can take
it any way it suits you."

Finley came back and sat on the sofa arm and took
a deep drink of his whiskey. "What I'm getting at—if
that's the case, we ought to be—I mean my wife and I
—realistic about all this. You agree?" Fargo did not
reply. "We ought to sit down and—"

"And what?" Fargo asked. "Bargain?"

Finley nodded, eyeing the front door.

"Bargain," Fargo said, and smiled with even white
teeth, but the smile quickly soured and he kicked at

the brown horse's mane. "You rich-ass niggers in the suburbs give me a pain. Bargain. Your bargaining days are—"

"Fascists," Olga interrupted, directing her hissing attack more at the back of Hedda's neck than at Fargo at the mantel. "See, Finley, they are Fascists, too! Just like the Black Circle people we read about in the *Times*. See, Finley, I knew it, I knew it."

"You uptight bitch," Fargo said, scarcely looking at her, "why don't you shut up?"

Olga would not be stilled. She stood, fingering the tear in her dress. "But why us? We haven't done anything to you. I could understand it if we were white— and—and oppressive or something. Or—or—I mean, Finley and I both are full life members of the NAACP."

The silence was more vicious than a barrage of vituperations, more stinging then any insult: Hedda, sitting on the coffee table, stretched her hand to grasp air from the heavens, and then, slowly drawing her fingers together into a fist, she softly tapped her forehead as if to rid her mind of the irrelevance of and her distaste for what Olga had said; Fargo, his back to the mirror above the empty fireplace, smiled in exaggerated pity.

Their silence, their arrogant beauty made Olga feel clumsy and old, a feeling so foreign to her that she became, as she sat down on the sofa again, too disoriented to hear the words floating across the room between

Finley and Fargo. They were sparring with words, with phrases, as if they were boxers warming up for the main event. At one point she heard Fargo protest, shout out, "Like hell—we're revolutionaries, man!" and she heard Finley retort, "Plain gangsters, I say!" but most of the bartering of words went unregistered, for her fingers had again begun their fluttery jumping upon the silk of her lap, and she could hear only the arguments of the half-dead leaves in the September wind.

It could not be called a reverie, Olga Blake's state of perturbation, but its quality was akin to the mindless drifting of a reverie, where thoughts do not take root or connect. She sat on the sofa glassy-eyed, not listening as Finley pulled up chairs about the coffee table. The drone of words, the accusations and denials, were, had Olga listened, but cat-and-mouse moves in which the extortionists were assessing the victim's vulnerability and the victim was determining the extortionists' power to demand. Had she attuned her ears to the stumbling, evil negotiations, she would have also discovered that Finley, a stubborn victim, was manipulating financial truths and stalling for time.

But Olga did not listen; often she was guided by reason and logic, but intuition and instinct, out of inclination and habit, served her better. It was intuition that set her fingers trembling and made her feel that no amount of conferring and compromise would halt the ultimate crumbling of her world, would end the sacking of her domain; it was instinct that told her, like an eagle on a cliff with her brood, that mortal danger was near. A world, a domain, was indeed how Olga thought of her home, her life, her station, and this notion stemmed not so much from pretentiousness and vanity as it did from her desire to erase the memory of the degradations of the past.

She was particularly fond of saying, to friends or to anyone who would listen, "We have not always lived at the castle," and the irony of her announcement was sharper than most would suspect. Although her childhood home in Anniston, Alabama, was not a shack, the two-room unpainted frame house at the corner of Depot and Elm was only one step away from being one, and it was without question too small for her mother and four sisters. It was there, with her mother and four sisters, in Anniston, at ten years of age, that Olga's lifelong preoccupations began: dreams of her absent father, maintenance of her dignity, and protection of the skin of her hands.

In one way or the other, her whole early life centered around this trinity. As early as ten or eleven she could scarcely remember her father's face, having only a vague idea that he was a pale man with a long thin nose, who dropped in and out of the household, who one day left for good, they said for Memphis, to pass, they said, for white. His fading across a boundary of race seemed romantic to her in those days and not at all cruel and heartless, for more households than not were without a father, and her father, unlike so many others, had not been an ordinary deserter, but had, she thought, with admirable style hoaxed the whites and beat the system.

She daydreamed of her father often, and wondered if he felt daring and dashing, like a spy in an alien land, fearful of detection. She herself once toyed with the idea of faking an accent and trying to escape from Anniston life by leaving home and passing for white. But her sisters and mother (whose colors were nutmeg and cinnamon and ginger) could not play the game of passing, and they desperately needed her; having no father meant less fatback in the collard greens; it also meant that she, being the eldest, must, in her mother's absence, tend to her younger sisters' biddies and diapers. Her mother, forever off in the kitchens of whites, would get home way past dusk, and would, in place of an evening prayer, prod Olga to remember always: "Keep your dignity, chile, no matter how much filth you have to put your hands into. You understand that? Never no matter what you have to do, don't lose your dignity."

At eleven Olga missed her mother's meaning and interpreted "dignity" (in relationship to her mother's words about "filth" and "hands") as something to do with applying lotion to her hands following the scrubbing and rinsing of her sisters' urine-stained clothes.

Later, at Booker T. Washington Junior High, and at
George Washington Carver Senior High, she interpreted
dignity to mean that it was necessary to hold her head
high even if she could not (unlike Ernestine Johnson
and Alice Thurman and Dolores Filmore) afford lip-
stick and thin shimmery stockings. By the time she'd
gone to Alabama State Teachers College, she knew
well the dictionary meaning of dignity, but still after
her weekend jobs of scrubbing and mopping in Clover-
dale at the Portlands and the Folsoms, she would apply
late at night, almost maniacally, lotion and creams to
her hands, not as if to eradicate the callouses and blisters
but rather to massage away her weekend condition of
servitude.

Yet even after her used-up youth in a long series of
sloppy kitchens and sloppy bedrooms, even after she
married Finley and worked to get him through Meharry
Medical School, even after the painful days on 117th
Street, especially that April, that April 23, and long
after she'd finished making her down payment toward
a better life and had actually *arrived* at that better life,
in St. Albans, with her Bloomingdale lamps and her
furnishings from Sloane's, and Lucille, the day maid—
even after all that, she still fanatically tended her hands
with lotions and creams. These days, however, she made
her ministrations in private, like a secret drinker, for
Sophie had said during one of their fights, "For crissake, Mother, you need a psychiatrist—putting that junk

on your hands fifty times a day is like those neurotics who wash themselves for hours and hours."

Olga had hit her. Before she could stop herself, she had struck her, slapped her daughter as she would not have hit an insulting shopkeeper, or a vicious neighbor, and then had run to her bedroom to cry, where she, without realizing it until her tears had finished, had been all the while massaging her hands with the comforting secrets of Nutrea 7.

On the sofa, now, she clamped her trembling hands in her lap. It was more fear that Sophie would make a caustic remark than it was fear of a refusal from Fargo and Hedda that kept her from asking to go upstairs and apply lotion to still her disquieted hands. But suddenly it did not matter; Fargo had out his revolver, standing in front of the coffee table, pointing it toward the study door.

With a jolt, Olga became alert.

She'd missed something. She'd been hardly aware that Finley had risen from his chair at the coffee table and left the room. Before she could ask what was going on, Finley came back from the study with two yellow legal pads and, with a forced attempt at conviviality, said to Fargo, "For God's sake, put that thing away. What did you think—I'd come out with a tommy gun or something?" He dumped the pads on the coffee table and went to the cabinet and poured a drink. Instead of returning to the table, he went back toward the study.

"Hold it, man," Fargo said, pulling out his revolver again from beneath his dashiki, "what're you up to now?"

Finley held out his glass. It was filled with two jiggers of whiskey. "Some soda," he said, continuing on toward the study. "I don't really like this stuff without soda." As he reached the study door, he said, "I think I've got an extra bottle in here somewhere."

Fargo stood. In his left hand he held his drink, in his right he aimed the revolver. "Suit yourself, but remember if you come out of there with anything but a bottle of soda, you're gonna be one shot-up motherfucker. Dig?"

Olga caught Sophie's glance. They both knew Finley did not use soda with his drinks, that there was no soda anywhere in the house, and that at best the only thing at all to drink in the study was perhaps a bottle or so of red burgundy. The study, a blight on Olga's otherwise meticulously arranged household, served as a quick hiding place whenever unexpected visitors appeared or Olga was too tired to take something to the attic or to the basement where it belonged. Apart from Finley's desk and volumes of medical books, and books on boating, there were dozens of back issues of *The New York Times* Sunday magazine sections; a backgammon set, practically in the middle of the floor (which needed some missing pieces, or to be thrown out); there was an

abandoned buffet cloth that Olga had found much too
intricate to continue crocheting—besides, she'd lost the
directions; a folding cot intended for the Salvation
Army; two tennis rackets in need of catgut; a clumsy
umbrella stand; five red clay flowerpots; and an old but
extravagant magenta housecoat Olga had hastily slung
across some empty hatboxes.

Fargo and Hedda waited.

Olga and Sophie listened.

There was a bit of rattling and shuffling in a drawer,
and then there was silence.

There was a crash. A crash of glass. At the French
window. It was not until Fargo and Hedda had run to
the study that Olga was able to make the most likely
reconstruction: Finley, in haste, had carelessly yanked
open the glass and metal door to the veranda and the
glass panel had struck the knobby protrusions of the
umbrella stand.

He'd escaped! He was out!

"The bastard!" Hedda said, back at the study door
with Fargo, her hazel eyes wide, alert. "Oh, the bastard!"

They stood there, as losers, Hedda and Fargo. They
stood there. Sophie laughed and whirled about on the
rug. She ran to the piano and started the Mozart and
Olga smiled for the first time that evening. She listened
for a second to Sophie's music, and then she rose from
the sofa, calmly but with a thrilling sense of recovered
control.

"Now, my dears," Olga said, flinging her arms luxuriously wide, "there's really no point in staying, is there?" She suddenly and fervently wished for music of greater power; the sonatina was not really the music for a moment like this. But it didn't matter. Life had suddenly become ever so much better. "Is there?" she asked again, over the creamy legato of Sophie's playing. She spoke to their backs, for they stopped and stared, as if frozen, at the closed front door.

"Hmm? You had no idea my husband was made of such stuff, did you? Did you? Oh, yes, he's mild, he's no bully like you—I mean, he is a man of medicine, of breeding, *Mister* Fargo. You didn't suppose he'd let you push us around indefinitely, did you, Mr. Fargo? Hmm?"

Neither of them answered, or moved. Fargo did not even have his switchblade out.

"Now, I do think you ought to go. Go! Don't just stand there, for heaven's sake—unless you want—you know, he's already down the street at Scotty and Sybil's. And I know they're home because Sybil wanted to know if—for crying out loud, Sophie, must you keep up that tiresome thing?"

It, the music, had turned bad to her ears as fear and nausea began to fill her. But Sophie did not stop, nor could she herself end her tirade, for her tormentors would not go. "And—and your Committee," she continued, the feeling of triumph giving way to the dry choking of her throat, "why, you're a couple of low-class intimidating thugs, that's all you are. Gangsters. That's all. Gangsters."

Olga found that tears had started to run down her cheeks and her legs had become unsteady. She picked up somebody's drink, and more to be doing something than thinking the drink would help her, she swallowed it bravely, swiftly, determined to keep it down.

"Now go!" she said, hearing her voice rise. "Get your vulgar selves *out of my house!* Do you hear me? Do you—"

The door opened.

Finley was thrown into the foyer head first by a burly man with all the hair on his head shaved off. The man had on sunglasses. He wore an old-fashioned gray suit with padding in the shoulders, and a black turtleneck sweater. He, like Hedda and Fargo, had a tiny gold earring pierced into his left ear. And the wind, the wind racing around on the lawn—it was stronger than ever; it blew a few leaves into the house.

Fargo said, "Good work, Cheeter. Good work, baby."

(3)

FARGO HURN threw himself down on Olga's sofa. As he stretched, he made sure the scotch in his glass did not spill, and he made sure the stretch itself lasted long enough for the muscular grace of his legs and arms to be noticed. Fargo was vain. He used his body and his face in the way a homely man uses his wits, a fat man his jolliness: he knew that in most respects he was out of the game, or at best deep in left field. And he thought he knew why. Long ago he'd learned that being poor meant more than just being without money. He even believed, half seriously, that poverty was a virus, that it got into his tongue and made him speak in a certain way, that it got into his brain and made him have attitudes different from the cats with fat wallets. Attitudes. Attitudes about life. Attitudes about anything. It haunted him, this notion, for he knew that people who had money not only spoke well (said the right words, and said them at the right time), but their attitudes were different from his, and it angered him that he could not crack the secret. He tried. He watched people. He studied them. Imitated them. But the secret was slippery and subtle, and one day, perhaps to soothe his pride, he decided the whole attitude business was a big trick anyway, a meanly clever way of shutting him out.

When he'd convinced himself that he could not master the trick, he decided to make fun of it, smash it. In fact, if Fargo Hurn were backed against a wall and pressed for the truth, he probably would admit that he was more concerned with defying attitudes than with revolution or reform. However, pressed for the truth, he probably would not admit that the Committee was only a cover for some hard-core thuggery that started one hot summer night at Lenox Avenue and 110th Street in Benny Pratt's Bar around the corner from Zenobia's Bar-B-Q Pit.

Fargo stretched again. His khaki trousers outlined his penis, which, because of its length and heft, still, after twenty-eight years, pleased and comforted him. But no one looked at it; they were looking at his boots on the sofa. He'd expected Olga to go into a hornet's fit when he'd first stuck his boots into the cushions at the end of her sofa, but she'd held her tongue and just glared at him. Finley, who was tied waist and feet to a straight-back chair, also watched, waiting to see what Fargo would do, what he'd say. Fargo knew that the time was getting ripe: they were on edge, but he would slide into it casually; the money, the Fear Money as Benny Pratt called it, was the touchiest part of the operation. As for the rest—there'd be no problem about the stereo and television set. They were there. And he didn't expect to have any problems about the Blakes' cars outside in the garage; they would be driven away and stripped.

"Hasn't he, Fargo?" Hedda was saying for the second time, poking her cigarette and fingers toward Finley, but managing to accuse Fargo in the process. "He's got more guts than you gave him credit for, hasn't he?"

"Shut up, Hedda. Let him talk." Fargo put his glass on the coffee table and adjusted the cushions behind his head. "Well, come on, baby. Talk."

Finley, who no longer tugged at the ropes binding his legs and waist, said, "Just what in the hell am I supposed to say?"

"Say what you gotta say, man. It's your problem."

"Money?"

"If it's $10,000 worth. Otherwise you can—"

"Ten thousand dollars!" Olga stopped patting a Kleenex at her neck. "Are you mad?"

"Christ," Finley said, almost smiling, "you folks've got the wrong people. What do you think I am, a bank or something?"

"Or a church, maybe?" Sophie chimed in.

"It's your problem, baby." Fargo raised up on his elbow and looked at Sophie. "And no more smart-ass shit from you, you hear?"

Although he gave her a slow prowl up her skinny legs to her bony hips, and gazed at her small breasts, she did not seem put off nor did she relax the pinched muscles around her mouth.

"Now look," he said, sitting upright on the sofa, "I'm doing my job, see. I'm just doing what I'm s'pose to be doing. I can tell you, I can think of a whole lot better things to do than to spend my evening with a bunch of bushwa niggers in St. Albans." He took a large swallow of scotch and added, quietly, "And you better believe it."

"Then," said Olga, her hands on Finley's shoulders, "just walk right out that door. I swear we won't stop you. I swear it."

She was using that high-ass tone again, that attitude which curdled Fargo's blood and made him want to smash something.

"As a matter of fact," Olga added, "you can take the station wagon and drive right down—"

"Shut up!" He jumped off the sofa, dropping his half-empty glass, but Hedda caught it. He really felt like smashing up the place. Who did this bitch think she was? "Now just shut up, goddamn it," he said, kicking the teddy bear out of his way. "Listen—now you just listen a bit. Don't hand *me* none of that uppity-ass shit. That's the trouble with you bastards to begin with. You get here where there's grass and trees and get a couple of cars in your fucking garage and—Jesus, it's, it's you half-white bushwa sonsabitches that's keeping us down. You. You. You. With your hinkitified piss-elegant imitations of whitey. Now look, mister, I don't know whether you've got $10,000 cash on hand or not but I know fucking well you can get it, so don't hand me that—that—"

He put his foot on top of the coffee table. He pointed his knife, although it was closed, at Finley. "In East Orange, New Jersey, this jack-legged preacher with a Mark IV Continental and a swimming pool tried to hand us some bullshit about his funds was all tied up and like he didn't even have a pot to—"

"Thirty thousand, honey," Hedda put in. "Just like that." She snapped her fingers to show how quick "just like that" had been, and even though it was a lie, Fargo had to admire the conviction of it.

But it was his show and he didn't want her stealing it, so he said, "Quiet, Hedda. And—and—like I was saying, he—where's that book? Lemme show you what the Committee knows, man. So don't come on all phony 'bout how much you ain't—" He stopped, felt his left hip pocket, and pulled out a leather notebook, worn and oily-smooth. "Here. Here. That jack-legged preacher in Jersey—$30,000." He flipped over a smudgy page. "Here. Then this here Clarence H. Barnes up on the Hudson-on-the-something, near Garrison, New York.

A big token black advertising shit—$20,000." Fargo flipped three other pages and then turned back to one he'd passed. "And this big gambler dude, this numbers man in Freeport, Long Island—$70,000. And—and, baby, this list goes on and on, and each one of them bastards started out claiming they didn't have no bread. Every fucking one of 'em. So don't hand *me* no shit, baby. I've got the facts. I've got the facts here, dig?"

Fargo turned four or five more pages and then said, with his elbow resting on his knee, his booted foot in the middle of the coffee table, "And now it's your turn. Finley Rutgers Blake. Adelaide Lane. St. Albans. Forty-seven. Wife, Olga. Daughter—"

"And," Hedda said, coolly, pointing to the teddy bear, "that there piece of shit."

"A sleep-out maid," Fargo went on. "Three downstairs exits." He stopped and looked at Hedda. "What's that mean? Are there two fucking doors in that kitchen?"

"Hmmm huh. Basement too. Locked it."

"Okay, two downstairs—let's see. And a Gino . . . Guy-no . . ."

"Gynecologist," Finley said.

"Gyne—cologist? Man, what the hell is that? One of them doctors for children?"

"Holy shit, Fargo." Hedda allowed herself a brief smile. "You ain't got a bit of sense. That's not a kiddie doctor, that's a pussy doctor."

"A *pussy* doctor?"

Hedda leaned over Finley, her hands on her hips, and said, "That's what a gyno-thing is, ain't it, honey? A pussy doctor." Her remark sounded like a threat. She smiled again.

Olga, who'd sat on the edge of the piano bench, stood up. "But we don't—we don't have—have all that much money just around as if—"

"Sit down and shut up," Fargo said, without taking his eyes from the biography. "Private clinic and consultant at Mount Sinai." He looked up at Olga for a second and said, "That don't sound exactly like eighty-five a week to me." Then back from his book he read, "AT&T. IBM. General Motors. Martinique and Barbados, three weeks in—"

"All right, all right, all right," Finley said, shaking his head back and forth. Little beads of sweat blistered his lip. Fargo waited. Then Finley said, "What are you trying to prove? Just what? Even if I did have that much cash around—which I don't—d'you expect me to get it, tied up like this? Do you? Do you?"

Fargo closed the oily notebook and stuck it back in his pocket. "Don't lose your cool, baby. I know you don't have $10,000 just sitting round the house. Just relax, man, just relax."

Finley could not relax. Muscles in his smooth chocolate face began to pop and jump. Fargo wondered if he

were about to go into a stroke; he'd begun to look un-
healthy.

"But," Finley said, "but if that's what you're after—
I mean, what's the point of all this?"

"Them ropes?" Hedda asked.

"I mean, you tie me up in my own house to get $10,-
000 and—and I mean, what's the point?"

Fargo glanced at his watch and went to the liquor
cabinet for a refill. "Man, how many times do I have
to tell you, you ask too many questions. Drink, Hedda?"

Finley, fuming, turned his head toward Fargo at the
liquor cabinet. "But, Christ," he said, almost in a whine,
"what do you want? Money? My life? Or both? I mean,
if this is a holdup, you're bungling it badly. Fargo?
Fargo, look at me. How do you expect to get it? How?"

Fargo knew the Blakes wanted some logical answers,
but he also knew that to get Fear Money he had to do a
lot more shaking up than he'd done; there hadn't yet
been enough menace and mystery in the game. He'd
hardly even talked about the Committee. He hadn't
made them sweat enough.

"What is this for?" Fargo asked, changing the subject, putting down his drink and picking up the teddy
bear.

"Answer me, Fargo!" Finley shouted. He rocked in
the chair as though he thought he could break through
the ropes. "For Christ's sake, answer me!"

"You'll get your answers," Fargo said, smiling with those teeth he knew to be especially even, especially attractive. "Plenty soon, baby, plenty soon."

"I'll bet," Sophie said, folding her arms and standing. She began walking back and forth behind her father's chair. "It's obviously a vicious bluff," she said in her prep-schooly voice. "Let's face it, there's no so-called Committee to begin with. Isn't that so? Isn't it?"

"Sophie," Finley said.

"But, Daddy," she said, racing fingers through her hair, "let's *do* face it. They kill us or they don't. Dead we're no good to them. And murder isn't all that easy to get away with. I mean, it wouldn't do their racketeering any good, would it? Right?"

Fargo watched her sit on the piano bench and cross her thin thighs. Squeeze that precious twat, he thought, let her squeeze it.

"Right, Fargo? And $10,000—poof! What are you going to do—march mother and daddy down to the Chase Manhattan at gun point and—oh, for crissake, put him down! Put Teddy down!" She ran over and tried to pull the bear out of his hands.

"Ah-ha, Baby Cunt's back in the arena again. What kind of bag you in, anyway? Like, what's a grown-up broad like you doing with a thing like this?"

"Why don't you let it alone? It doesn't belong to you."

"Is that a fact?" Fargo squeezed Teddy's thick arms,

his stomach. "But look at this sonofabitch. There's enough teddy here for fifty teddy bears."

"So? So? What do you want me to do? Cut him up in pieces and dole him out to the Poverty Program?"

"Maybe. As a matter of fact, smart-ass, that may be just the thing you oughta do." He took out his knife, pressed the black button on the case's side, and the blade shot out, catching yellow glints from the table lamp. "Huh?"

"No!"

"Why not?"

"No, no . . . please. You wouldn't . . . I mean, it's only a ted—"

"Why not?"

"No, no, please."

"Why not?"

"You—you mustn't."

"No?" he asked and at the same time plunged the long blade into the bear's belly. Sophie bent forward and held her stomach. He stabbed the bear a second time. And then another time. The fourth time the blade went into the furry stomach, Sophie bit hard into her fist.

"This stupid piece of crap," he said, watching Sophie bite her fist as he twisted the knife around in the brown fur. "This stupid piece of crap. Why did you get this stupid piece of crap? Why did you get it? Huh? Tell me."

"Teddy. Tedd . . ." Sophie said, softly.

"Aw, cut it out."

"You . . ."

"I said, cut it out!"

Olga rose and attempted to rescue the bear. "You are inhuman . . . a harmless little teddy."

"*Little?*" Hedda said.

"Get back," Fargo said, and threw the bear on the floor. "Leave it where it is."

"But—"

"Leave it, Mrs. Bitch!" Fargo waited for Olga to step back, then to Sophie he said, "What *is* this bullshit with this goddamn teddy bear? You hear me talking? Answer me."

Sophie hadn't cried but her eyes were watery, glazed. "I—it's a present. I've had it for a long time. I've always had it, Teddy. And you—you stabbed Teddy. You—" She stopped and bent to pick the bear up.

"Leave it on the goddamn floor." They both looked down at Teddy on the rug, his pink eyes staring cold-glass back up at them. "Jesus. So I stabbed a hunk of cotton. A big fat hunk of goddamn cotton and rags. Jesus. Hedda, fill me up again. Some more of that boss Chivas Regal."

Hedda picked up his glass, which was still pretty full, and dumped the contents into the potted fern next to the magazine rack. As Olga drew in a sudden sharp breath, Hedda turned and said with a cold clip, "Vitamins." Then to Finley she said, "You drinking, buster?"

"How'd you expect me to drink if I'm tied up like some—"

"Aw," Hedda said, stopping in front of Finley's chair, "cool it, will you? You do a lot of whining, it seems to me."

". . . It wasn't that I always had Teddy," Sophie was saying. It was like she'd had a shot of morphine, Fargo thought, or was talking in her sleep. She spoke in a quiet singsongy tone and her glassy eyes stared at the bear at her feet. "Once, once I didn't. Once, one August before I was . . . it was a birthday, I think, or maybe it was for—"

"Sophie." Olga's lips quivered. "Now, Sophie, you're —you're distraught, dear. Why don't you sit down for a minute . . . and Teddy will be . . . oh, Sophie, please stop staring at him like that! Sit down!"

"What's this fucking teddy-bear hangup?" Fargo asked. "You'd think—"

"There was a staircase in that house, I think," Sophie said. "Or did I have Teddy then?" She frowned at the bear at her feet.

"Sophie," Olga said, "please, Sophie, sit down and have a drink. Finley, oughtn't she take a drink? Please. This is merely going to—"

"Button up, bitch," Fargo said, and nudged the bear with his foot. "And? And?"

Sophie rubbed her elbow. She looked around the room

as if she didn't recognize it. "You stabbed him. You stabbed him."

Sophie's voice sounded buried in her throat and her eyes looked as glassy as the bear's. Fargo watched her closely but he couldn't—he couldn't *get through* to her.

"I'm going to pick him up now," she said, softly, "and I don't care what you do."

For a minute he thought neither one of them was talking about Teddy, but they must be talking about Teddy, he decided, because if they weren't talking about Teddy, what *were* they talking about?

Sophie bent down slowly.

"Don't pick him up," Fargo said, wondering if his own eyes looked as glassy as Sophie's, as Teddy's, but wondering mostly why he didn't just walk over to the other side of the room and look out of the window or clean his nails or something.

Sophie picked up the teddy bear.

"Shit, shit, good Jesus, it's just a hunk of rags and cotton and junk, your Teddy. What sort of fucking bag you tryin' to put *me* in? Do you—do you want me to kiss the fucker to make it all right, huh? To make the hurt go away, huh? Jesus almighty." He was shouting but she did not seem to hear him.

"Yes."

"Yes?"

"Yes."

"Yes, what?"

"Kiss him. Kiss him to stop the hurt."

"Come on, now . . . you gotta be kiddin'."

"Kiss him. Here. Here. Here where you stabbed him."

"I didn't stab him—I mean, I stabbed him but I didn't—didn't—"

"Kiss him. Kiss him to stop the—"

"No! Jesus, no. Don't put that thing in my face, you hear? Get back!"

"Kiss him, Fargo. You bully. Kiss him."

"I didn't . . . didn't—look, how was I to know that—"

"Kiss him!"

Fargo found the teddy in his arms. He felt the scotch rising to his head. ". . . It's just a teddy bear," he heard his voice saying; he'd been talking and hadn't heard all of what he'd said and before he could look away from the pink glass of the bear's eyes and before the scotch left his head he'd buried his face into the bear's belly and kissed its wounds.

"*Jesus* H. Christ, Jr.," Hedda said.

Olga's knifing laughter cut through Fargo's fuzziness. Her squeal as she spun around in a circle and sank down upon the sofa shot up in his ears like icicles. She sat there, her head flung back, laughing with a mouthful

of teeth, her pale face turning the color of beets. She
pounded her hands together in joy. "You kissed him.
She made you kiss him. She made you . . ."

Fargo slapped Olga's laughing face as hard as he'd ever
hit a woman—as hard as he would hit a man. His hand
stung from the slap he'd landed across her grinning face,
but the swing of his arm, the contact across her cheek
cleared his head, dried up the scotch; he'd cut her off,
cleanly, in the middle of her laugh. There suddenly was
no sound in the room. No sound anywhere except for
the wind in the garden. When he could get back his
breath, when he could speak, he said, "So what if I did,
you cunt."

Finley, bound in his chair, attempted to hopscotch
along the rug toward Olga, but Hedda's slim leg blocked
him. "Relax, doll," she said, "you ain't going nowhere."

Fargo was beyond immediate help. Smashing the glass
sea gull over the brown horse's head didn't help. Fargo
ground some of the shattered glass into the stones of the
hearth with his heel, but that didn't help. Tearing up
the room wouldn't help; there wasn't enough in the
room to tear up to help. His back was to them. He spoke
into the empty fireplace, grinding to ashes pieces of the
broken sea gull. "I don't know why I'm even fucking
around with you sonsabitches to begin with. I should've
made my say and had Cheeter wait in here. Oh, but
you're gonna get yours—you—you bushwa bastards.
You're going to pay, pay, pay, pay for everything."

He turned from the fireplace and looked at them, at the Blakes—sitting in a row like three teddy bears. "Believe me, you're going to pay for keeping me, for keeping us down. For every dirty red morning on every Harlem street in every Harlem part of this country, you're going to pay. For every time you and the likes of you spread your dust from your El Dorados and your Continentals going to—to wherever the hoity-toity shit you motherfuckers go . . . drinking your fine booze . . . being foxy in your fine furs . . . you're going to pay."

He began walking around, but there wasn't enough space for his legs, not enough room. He tilted lampshades, knocked pictures crooked, flipped up doilies, knocked Teddy sideways in his chair.

"Goddamn it, *I* didn't have me no teddy bear—not even a little ratty teddy bear. I was fucking lucky to have a top."

He bent down and shouted into Sophie's face, "A spinning top, I was lucky to have," but she did not move. Then, back at the empty fireplace with a foot on top of one of the horse's backs, he said, "But your time's now, you smug sonsabitches. The Revolution is beginning, baby, it's beginning and you and your kind gotta be the *first* to go. The *first*, baby. Not whitey, baby. Whitey's too big to bat down all at one time but you sonsabitches ain't. You ain't! And $10,000, ha! That's a small price to pay if you wanna know—"

"But . . ." Olga started, raising her arm, her bird-neck taut.

"Shut up, you hear?" His hand found a glass goblet and threw it like a baseball, the goblet finding its mark on a panel near the study door. No one turned to look at it. No one moved. "Believe me—I mean, man, you're getting off cheap, if you ask me. When I think of them kids I see every day, kids I know, like I used to be, in one crumbled-down room with no plaster and no heat and no food and no way to stop the rats—have you ever *seen* rats? Real fat big rats? Ever heard 'em across from your bed in the dark?"

Fargo sat down on one of the porcelain horses at the hearth. For a time he looked at the pale rug, and when he spoke again his words came quietly, sometimes in a whisper. "I think of all them rats and then I see you black-half-white bushwa smug fuckers throwing a few peanuts to that Uncle Tom-ing NAACP and thinking you done your deed for the season—why, man, it makes me want to—you know what I mean? Man, you don't know what I mean. You don't even know why you—you —all you black Anglo-Saxon fuckers gotta be the *first* to go in this Revolution. You know that? You know that?" Fargo saw that Sophie was about to speak but he cut her off. "*You* our *first* enemy, baby. You been keepin' us down more'n whitey ever kept us down, you know that? No, you don't know that."

He got up from the brown horse and went toward

the liquor cabinet, and then he changed his mind. He banged three times on a cluster of black and white keys as he began again to stride around the room, around Teddy's chair, up and down before the study door. "Y'awl don't know from shit. None of you fancy niggers do. But you will learn, baby, you will learn."

His fingers pointed to Olga, who'd followed his walk about the room, with eyebrows raised and her neck stiff. "And you, you uptight, dry-assed cunt, you needn't look so snide, like I'm just full of talk—reparations, baby, is what I'm talking about and it's easier than you'd think. It's already worked dozens of times, I can tell you. Dozens of times."

Nobody said anything. The echo of Fargo's words rang in their ears.

Fargo leaned over the back of Teddy's chair—Teddy was sitting sideways, his pink eyes staring at the floor. In a cool voice, he said, "Like, all we need is a written promise you'll pay the price on your head." There weren't any takers, so he said again, "Just the price on your head. And we'll tell you how and where." He listened to the silence again, the breathing.

They waited for him to go on but he held off for a moment; he could almost taste their fear. Then he said, "And another thing, you can't even move or get out of the country without the Committee knowin' it. You know that? And the Committee is patient. Real patient. I mean, maybe like sometimes *too* patient." He leaned forward and stared at Olga. "You think we're bluffing? Okay, say we leave. Six months from now you're sure we were bluffing until one day you get a hat pin stuck in your neck—under a dryer in the beauty parlor."

Olga quickly pressed a hand to her throat.

"And you, man. You're taking yourself a nice swim in Barbados or Trinidad or wherever the fuck you go —you know, like even way next summer—and, you know, you may never come up again out of that water." Fargo extracted the oily black notebook again. "Look, I gotta list *that* long of bushwa niggers who thought we was bluffin' and didn't pay up." He flipped through some back pages of the small notebook. "The Committee just got one cat last week in a washroom. Down near Wall Street. They planted a janitor down there who waited three months to get the cocksucker. Acid. All over his fucking face. And think I'm kidding if you want."

A feeling of power swelled up inside him but at the same time he felt cheated, for he wanted to *see* himself acting, playing his role. He would have liked to have had his speech taped, so that he might listen to himself.

Fargo dumped Teddy on the floor and sat in the chair himself, stretching his legs out, resting them, his heels on the rug. He saw everybody looking at him, even Hedda, looking at his crotch. He knew that the thin khaki trousers revealed the outlines of his cock, but he was surprised they all stared at it. After a moment their gaze forced him to look down into his lap—and, goddamn, his fly was open! He zipped up quickly. Too quickly. That small quick gesture took away some of the pleasure he'd been feeling about his heavy talk. Life was treacherous; it was little traps like that which got under his skin—he really wished he hadn't zipped up so fast—but he went on, speaking quickly, "And I can tell you it don't matter if you get out the FBI and the State troopers and the CIA and the whole fucking Marine Corps 'cause you don't know *where* and *who* the Committee is, and it ain't no way for you to find out, baby."

Fargo stopped talking. He decided to lower his voice and speak with less fire. He wasn't sounding as sinister as he'd hoped. He also found it was not easy to wipe away the real image of the Committee, for Zenobia's Bar-B-Q Pit and Benny Pratt's Bar kept seeping back into his mind. Zenobia and Benny Pratt. They, with their holes-in-the-wall, were not Fargo's idea of king-pins—yet he could not put them down; they had the ways and means; he was, when he got down to it, only in their hire.

Zenobia's Bar-B-Q Pit looked exactly like a hundred other fish-frying holes in Harlem. Her place, with moldy barbecue in the window, was on St. Nicholas Avenue near 110th Street. Benny Pratt's Bar was right around the corner. Both places were greasy firetraps, but it made Fargo's head swim whenever he thought of all the money that rolled into those joints. Dope money. Stolen-car money. Numbers money. And now with the Committee in operation, with three other squads besides Hedda and Cheeter and himself—well, who was he to put Benny and Zenobia down?

Fargo looked over to see what Finley had begun to sputter about; he'd started twisting in his seat and shaking his head like he was about to come on with some new bullshit.

"Fargo," Finley said, "listen to me. Listen for a minute. What do you think you're going to get away with? Come on, now. Even murder isn't as easy as you make it out, you know. Getting away with it, I mean. It seems to me actually that—"

"Who's gonna stop us? Huh? And who's gonna hunt us down? I hope you ain't referrin' to protection from whitey." Fargo stood up and began pacing up and down behind the sofa. "You think whitey really gives a good fuck about protecting you, baby? Even as half white as you are? Oh, yeah, they'll come around and go through a lot of bullshit, but afterward, know what they say behind your back? You don't know about cops, I bet, do you? You know what they say? I mean, like at the precinct? They say 'A dead nigger is just one less nigger,' that's what they say. And they've been saying that for years, baby. *Years!* I mean, like this pretty rug here, and that brand-new Pontiac out there, and all this other shit you got don't cut no ice with the pigs, man. Like Malcolm said—and you oughta read Malcolm

X—it just might clear up your head—but like he said, 'Down at the precinct, a Ph.D. is still a nigger.' And don't you forget it.—What's that?"

"What's what?" Hedda said.

"That noise."

"Noise? What kind of noise?"

"I thought I heard—"

"Maybe Cheeter."

Olga sprang up to look at the clock near the staircase. "Maybe it's—Finley, did Sco—"

"Olga." Finley shifted his eyes from the right to the left, then back to his knees.

Fargo walked to the door and eased it open. When he saw Cheeter in the yard down near the umbrellas, he closed it again. "Yeah, must be Cheeter." He then made himself another drink. "Have you been understanding anything I've been saying? Huh?"

"Suppose," Finley said, "suppose I say no, right now. Then what?"

"We're s'pose to *convince* you, man." Fargo left the liquor cabinet and went to the fireplace to watch himself drink in front of the looking glass above the mantel. "What do you think me and Hedda're here for?"

Finley turned his head toward Fargo at the mantel. "That's what I mean. Say you don't convince us. Then what? You shoot us? Here on the spot?"

A small cry broke from Olga's shaking mouth. "They said midnight, Finley. I heard them say midnight."

"Naw, naw," Fargo said, looking at Olga in the mirror. "Shoot you for what? Unless you get outta hand. Like I said, the Committee does the killing when and where and how they decide it. Dig?"

Olga and Finley made no comment. The room was quiet again. Fargo then looked at the sideburns he was attempting to grow. It took so long for them to come down, really down, as far as he wished they would come, but his hair had grown quickly and he was pleased that it had shaped up so well. Everyone said his new Afro made him look like an actor. And he wouldn't mind if he had become an actor. He knew he was better-looking than any one of the black actors he saw in a show in Greenwich Village once. Any one of them. Except maybe one. But it was too late. It was too late to be an actor, and it was too late to pick up from the tenth grade, and it was too late for everything except loading dresses on trucks, or sticking books into boxes, or saying "More coffee, sir?" But it wasn't too late for Benny and Zenobia, even if he was a low card in their deck, and in a way, his job for Benny was a sort of acting job; it was almost like being an actor. Almost.

Then, something happened.

At first he couldn't quite put his finger on it, for the scotch had been rushing to his head as he stood at the mantel before the mirror, and he'd been too wrapped up in himself to be quick on the uptake. He'd been standing here, facing the mirror with his drink resting on the mantelpiece. He'd turned his face to the left, to make a profile, and had with slow eyes traced the perfect shape of his Afro haircut. And then next he'd traced with half-closed eyes, from his forehead to his nose, the shape he thought so suitable to be seen on a stage. It was just about when his eyes reached the line of his upper lip that he saw (not *saw* exactly, at first, but rather *felt*) another presence, another person in the mirror.

His eyes left the curve of his upper lip and shifted to the right corner of the mirror. Olga. At some distance behind him, Olga, one hand fluffing her flouncy hair and the other hand pressing her bird-neck, had been looking at herself with a frown, as if in the mirror only her own face registered. But she, too, had suddenly shifted her eyes, and they met his, almost as if by accident. They both had been caught in the act: Fargo had seen how frightened Olga was of getting old; she seemed to hate the wrinkles about her neck, a neck that must have once been as smooth as Sophie's; but she, she had seen him, too.

Olga looked away.

Fargo picked up his drink.

"Hey! Hey, Fargo." It was Cheeter. At the front door. He'd burst in panting.

"What—?" Fargo put his drink on the mantel. "What's up?"

Cheeter was beefy. He was sweating, even his sunglasses were sweating. "Look—I know you ain't going to believe this, man, but some cocksucker is coming . . . is coming up the—"

"Shit. Close the door. Coming here?"

"I mean, I know you gonna think I'm out of my mind . . . but . . . but some cat's down there at the end of the yard coming up here—I mean, heading toward here with—"

"Here?" Hedda said, springing over to bolt the door. "He alone?"

"Yeah. By hisself. The cat's gotta—a—a *doo*dad. One of these here lawn things—you know, like 'putt-putt.' . . . He's heading straight up this way."

"You sure?" Fargo felt for the butt of his revolver. "And he's alone?"

"He just started up from the bottom gate . . . coming this way . . . singing his fool head off . . . and with that putt-putt thing."

Olga sprang to her feet. "It's Scotty! With the power mower!" She ran toward the front door, calling, "Scotty! Sco—"

Hedda clamped her hand over Olga's mouth. "Shut up, bitch!—Jesus, Fargo, whatta we going to do now?"

Cheeter said, "Want me to shoot him?"

Fargo glanced at his watch. "You crazy? Friend of yours, Finley? Huh? Who is it, motherfucker?"

Finley said, "FBI agent."

The back of Fargo's hand slashed across Finley's face. "*Who?*"

"A neighbor! A neighbor, for God's sake. I *do* have neighbors, you know."

"What's that noise?" Fargo asked.

"The 'putt-putt,'" Hedda said. "Whyn't you let Cheeter get him?"

"Shut up. I'm running this. Come on. Everybody in there." He pointed to Finley's study. "Everybody! Drag him in, Cheeter— chair and all. And stuff a fucking rag in his mouth."

Cheeter tilted Finley back on two legs of the straightback chair and slid him across the rug into the study. Fargo held Sophie and Olga. The noise of the power mower stopped. "Here, you take her," Fargo told Cheeter, pushing Olga forward, "and hold the bitch's mouth." Fargo then took Sophie by the waist, lifted her off the floor, with one hand pressed across her face. The doorbell rang. "Now, look, Hedda, get rid of the cocksucker. Do anything. Don't let him get no ideas. Don't—"

"But do *what?*"

"*Anything,* damn it. Tell 'em, tell 'em—just get rid of 'em."

"Fin!" The shout from outside was accompanied with a jazzy, jerky jolt of the bell. "Fin, you old buzzard, open up."

"Okay, Hedda?" Fargo pulled Sophie into the study with Cheeter and Olga and Finley. "Okay?"

(4)

A L T H O U G H   M O S T people thought otherwise, Hedda Brewster had been to bed with only three men in her life. As she opened the door, Scotty Sykes must have thought otherwise, too; he ogled. He was a thin, ginger-colored man with brown freckles splattered across his face. It seemed to Hedda that he smelled of peppermint and lime.

"Oh. Who are you? I mean, is Fin here? Dr. Blake?"

Hedda hadn't had time to decide who she would be. Right away she ruled out the idea of trying to pass herself off as a friend or a distant cousin. She thought it safest to pretend to be a maid and gave the man an unfriendly "No, sir, they went out. They're gone." She knew she'd sounded a bit tough so she quickly watered it down with: "Can you leave a message, please?"

"A message? I'm—I'm just down the—" He stopped. He pressed his tongue into the top row of his teeth, and looked across her shoulder at the glasses, the lazy blue cigarette smoke, the mess in the room. "Did those sneaks have a party here tonight?"

Before she could answer, he, smiling, pushed on past

her as if it were his God-given right, and then walked
down two steps into the living room. "I bet those sneaks
did, I bet they did," he said, laughing, picking up
glasses and sniffing at them, making himself at home.
"It's funny. Fin said he'd be around. What happened?
Where'd they go? Where's Lucille?"

"Lucille?"

"Yeah," Scotty Sykes said, fingering pieces of the
smashed sea gull. "Lucille. Their day help. You're—"
He turned to Hedda. "Who're you again? Sorry, I didn't
catch your name."

Before she could stop herself, Hedda had put her
hands on her hips and said, "I'm Miss Brewster." When
he blinked and cocked his head to the side, she dropped
her hands from her hips and said quietly, "Hedda. I'm
helping out for Lucille." His eyelids (even his eyelids
had freckles on them) lowered as he took in the curves
of her legs in her pink-tinted stockings. When his eyes,
the color of ripe olives, began a slow rise upward, Hedda
swung around and headed for the kitchen. "Look, just
a second and I'll get you some paper and a pencil."

"I—"

But she'd left. She stood by the kitchen sink. She was
certain there was paper and pencil in the living room
somewhere but she had gone into the kitchen to be
alone for a second, to cool off. The uppity bastard, she
thought—taking her for granted like that! She knew
well enough she was capable of exploding, and once she

started exploding there'd be no end to it, even if she destroyed herself along the way. That, in fact, had been her history—destroying herself as she did her foe in. With Jake Foster, the first man she'd slept with (and her husband for five days), that had been the case. She was still in Benjamin Franklin High School when she'd become pregnant with Jake's child, and for two years afterward she chased him, sugarcoated him, slept with him (as an unwed mother), until he finally—he'd not been mean; he was just young and no-good—gave in and married her. The revenge was bitter and it was sweet: as soon as she got home from the wedding, she started divorce proceedings. She'd trapped him, married him, and then got even. She handed over the baby to her mother-in-law, who didn't mind a bit because she had some weird thing about wanting to be a grandmother. Jake Foster was, as she'd hoped, frightened and hurt and done in: his male vanity would not let him believe those two years of lovemaking (out of wedlock, after the child was born) were a cold, calculated two-year scheme to marry him and divorce him.

"Hey," Scotty Sykes called out from the living room. "I don't need any paper or anything. I mean, I don't want to write a message or anything."

"Be right with you," Hedda called back, running the tap to get a glass of water. *The goddamned bastard. Where does he get off shouting "hey" like that? Does he think I'm some sort of piece of shit or something?*

That "hey" sounded a lot like Benny. Benny Pratt.
Benny went around shouting "hey" at people.

Hedda had been in love with Benny Pratt. For a
number of years after her cold-knife revenge on her five-
day husband, the idea of sleeping with a man repelled
her. She was happy to be a loner for a while, on her
own, with no ties whatsoever. Now and then she found
she had to make it with her hand, but even then it was
a nothing act, like gargling or blowing her nose; she
did it merely to quiet feelings that rose up against her
will. Then there was Benny. Benny Pratt. She'd been a
cocktail waitress in Tiggy's, on Seventh Avenue near
137th Street, one of Benny Pratt's establishments. There
were a lot of fancy mirrors at Tiggy's and a lot of fake
brick walls and it was phony through and through, but
it was a job, and she was fascinated with Benny and his
chartreuse automobile, his diamond rings, his funny
pointed shoes. Also, she did not kid herself: she enjoyed
the extra benefits of dating the big boss.

Then one night, in an apartment on Convent Avenue,
he took off his rings, his shiny suit, his yellow pointed
shoes. As he shed his possessions, his crude jokes and his
brassy boasting also disappeared. Hedda found Benny
Pratt no more than an aging man with a paunch, with
calves too skinny for his heavy thighs, with beefy shoulders, with a set of bad teeth (the whole upper left part
of his teeth was false). It might have been then, when
he shed his glitter, that she fell in love with him; it was

much later that she began to hear the rumors that Zenobia, Zenobia the owner of the evil-smelling Bar-B-Q Pit on St. Nicholas Avenue, was his wife.

"But *where?*" Scotty Sykes asked again. He stood in the kitchen door behind her. "I just talked to Fin on the phone—oh, maybe, you know, not too long ago."

Hedda whirled around and lashed out. "They left, I told you. I don't ask my employers their business. How the hell am I suppose to know?"

"I beg your pardon." His brown freckles turned darker as his words drew an imaginary line between them.

Hedda adjusted her earring and walked out of the kitchen. "I'm sorry, I'm sorry. Excuse me. I'm—I'm— look, mister, I'm uptight about all this. Cleaning up all this. I don't do it much. And I've got to go."

She knew, she *felt,* even with her back turned, that he was watching her walk, and when she turned to look around, she saw that his ogling was working to her advantage: he was not concerned about the insult; fuck was on his mind. Hedda was both miffed and pleased. On one hand, she hated always being reduced to a sex machine, but also she liked the feeling of power it gave her.

"I bet," Scotty Sykes said, following her across the room, "it's Olga's mother. Hell, I bet the poor woman's . . ." He picked up the phone and raised his forefinger to dial.

"No, no!" Hedda almost yanked the phone from his hands. "I mean, it's not Mrs. Blake. Nothing's wrong with Mrs. Blake."

"You mean Mrs. Simpson—Olga's mother."

"Yeah, yeah, that's what I mean." She began picking up ashtrays, even clean ones. "You know, I freelance around so much . . . all these names . . ." She took two ashtrays and three glasses to the kitchen. When she returned, she said, "I hope you don't think I'm rude or anything like that, but I've got to clean. I mean, I've got to get out of here to get to the F train. You know—at 179th Street. So why don't you—"

"Look," he said, staring at her breasts again, "they almost never go out." He picked up the phone. "I'm sure that—look, I'm going to call—"

"But they're not—"

"—my wife."

With temporary relief, Hedda went back to the kitchen and ran water in the sink. She found soap powder and splashed a dollop over the glasses and ashtrays. She was playing maid. She hated being forced into a role. Any kind of role. With Benny Pratt she'd been forced into one, in a way. When she'd found out he was married (though he'd never say whether it was Zenobia or not), she found herself in the role of Benny's Girl. Benny's Girl—half of Harlem called her that. Then at last, after many false starts and lots of pep talks to herself, she got up enough nerve to say one evening,

"Look, Benny, we ought to call this thing off. You know? What I mean is, there's no future in it for me. You know?"

She'd been cool about it, hip, just as she'd practiced, but she had never dreamed that his flippant, jolly "thata girl" would shake her so. *Thata girl!* She couldn't even cry. She could hardly speak. She nearly vomited. The arrogance! He'd made love with all the tenderness, with all the lies, with all the valentine gush in the book, and then in the end he said "Thata girl" as if she'd been an empty carton of milk, an old tin can, an empty package of cigarettes.

It would have been different had he been trying to get rid of her, and she'd finally come around to his point of view. But they'd never talked about splitting. In fact, she thought she was being sensible and brave. Then he came up with his easy, offhand "thata girl." The sound of his words rang in her ears for months.

Hedda's decision to put her strength and resolve to trial finally drove her to Benny Pratt's Bar on Lenox Avenue near 110th Street. She felt there was only one test to see if she really had gotten rid of Benny, gotten him out of her blood; she had to see him face to face and feel no pangs about it. Although she knew that Benny rarely showed up in his Lenox Avenue bar, it didn't matter; it was something to do; she was lonely. And the noisy bar, with its whores and pimps and addicts, never really bothered her much, either—she was not interested in any of that. Her new title, Benny Pratt's Ex-Girl Friend, protected her. She was left alone, for no one was certain how much power an ex-girl friend had.

That night she met Fargo in the bar. Fargo Hurn. He stepped up to the stool beside her, apparently having seen her around, and said, "You foxy bitch, you. What's your bag? Drink?" That had been the beginning. That started it.

"Sybil," Scotty Sykes was saying, "Sybil's the missus." He was off the phone and leaning on the refrigerator watching Hedda make suds in the sink. He seemed very relaxed. Too relaxed. "Sybil's got a lot of hangups," he said. "You know what I mean?"

Hedda didn't know and she didn't care. She only regretted Fargo was behind the study door, within hearing range; otherwise, it would have been easy enough to handle Mr. Scotty Sykes.

When Hedda did not answer, he said, "What do you do? I mean, off duty, when you're not substituting."

So, there it was. Out in the open. The bastard. But Hedda said, "You making a pass at me, buster?"

"Oh, no. No, no. Sorry. What I meant was, is this your regular job? Filling in for—well, I suppose you're filling in for Lucille, aren't you?"

"What's it look like I'm doing?"

"That's what I meant, really. That's what I meant."

He stammered. He shifted his elbow on the refrigerator top and began rattling a large box of kitchen matches. "What I meant, really, was that you don't look—I mean, see, well, I just wondered . . . Look, Sybil—and Sybil, like I said, is the missus down the block—Sybil and Olga plan to go to Atlantic City next week for some sort of—oh, the National Negro Women's Council or some sort of thing. I was thinking—I mean, since you substitute—I mean, our girl, Mamie, has a—has a vacation in Winston-Salem, and for a week I'll be needing . . . You suppose you could come down the street? It's just a good block down the way—I mean, through Olga and proper and everything, if you want and—and . . ."

Hedda looked at him. It took her a long time to get it out, but when she did she said it plain enough: "Why don't you go home?"

"Now—now—I didn't—"

"I know fuck-talk when I hear it, buster. You think just because—because—oh, Christ, go home!"

Although he stopped smiling, his hands seemed happy. They seemed to be juggling something invisible in the air. His freckles slid around his face. "Well, I guess I'd better fix me a drink on top of that." Then he suddenly said, "What's that?"

There was a noise, a bump in the study, but Hedda quickly said, "I didn't hear nothing."

"From there," Scotty Sykes said, pointing toward the

study. "I'd've sworn . . . You didn't hear anything?"

"It's getting nippy. The wind. Specially out here with the trees and—" There it was again! Hedda wondered what they were doing in there.

"Could be," Scotty Sykes said, going toward the study, "that the window is—"

"Unh huh." Hedda just barely managed to get herself in front of the door, in front of him, but after she'd managed that maneuver, it then seemed like a dead giveaway. Now she had to perform. "Ahhh, you sly bastard, you," she said, tapping his stomach and feeling sick with the thought that Fargo now could hear everything she said, "you trying to make me afraid, aren't you? You a big tease. How'd you know I'm afraid in big old houses alone? Hmm?"

When Hedda pressed her left breast into his arm, he said, "I—well, I—"

"Have you got a big old house, honey? Down the street there?"

"It's—it's fairly large, I guess you'd say. It's—"

"And when does she go? To Atlantic City, your wife?"

"Oh, you *would* come? Would you really come?"

"Depends," Hedda said, easing him away from the door, pulling him piecemeal. "Depends on a lot of things."

"Like on what?" Scotty Sykes acted like a starved rat. "I'd make it—it, you know, worth your time. And—and

you wouldn't have to go back to the city if you didn't
want to—I mean, there's a spare room if it's convenient
for you to—"

"Sleep overnight? Huh? Now, that's a little much,
isn't it? What would your wife say—I mean about my
staying overnight in your house?"

"She'll be in Atlantic City, I'm telling you."

"Is it a lot of work—at your house?"

"How much work do you want?"

"How much can you afford to pay for?"

His lips began to glisten and his hand moved toward
her breast. Hedda dodged. "Look, buster, finish up that
drink and I'll write my phone number down, okay?
Then you're getting your ass out of here, you understand?"

As Scotty Sykes quieted his lechery with brandy,
Hedda searched for a pencil. There'd been several
around in the living room earlier in the evening, but
somewhere in the rumpus they'd been lost. She looked
under the sofa and in the magazine rack without luck.
In the kitchen, stuck to the side of the refrigerator with
a magnetic tape, she'd seen a small white pad of paper,
and she decided a pencil should be near. She dug around
in a kitchen drawer but only found some kitchen spoons,
a pair of pliers, a spatula, several can openers. She smiled,
wondering what false number she would give him—if
she could find a pencil—but her smile faded when she
thought of the last time she'd given out her number (her

real one). In Benny Pratt's Bar, Fargo eventually got around to asking for her phone number. She gave it to him. And that started it.

Fargo was the third man Hedda had ever slept with. It was the cancerous memory of Benny Pratt's "thata girl" that urged her to say to Fargo during the first night in the ash-gray light of his boardinghouse room as she undressed, "Fargo, don't make love to me, just fuck me." She was determined no longer to play the game men played—that I'll-love-you-forever song-and-dance they spouted prior to bedding down (and sometimes during), which, right after the last gasp of passion, turned into "Let's go out and get some pizza," or worse, when the affair was over, into "Thata girl." No, she intended to hurt before she got hurt; she intended to kill before any hurt could be done.

What she said stunned Fargo; even in the dark she could tell it upset him. He, like most men, couldn't handle a remark like that; he, too, needed to pretend love. Unfortunately Hedda, locked in her own terms, her own demand—just fuck, no love—fell in love with Fargo, and that was why she was here now, with Fargo behind the door, in the other room.

"Why's the door locked?" While Hedda had been rummaging through still another drawer, looking for even a stub of a pencil, Scotty Sykes had left his drink and had begun rattling the knob of the study door. "Why?" he asked again. "Fin never locks it."

"How the fuck am I suppose to know?" Hedda said. "Now, look, you're getting on my nerves. It's one thing if you're—"

"Mr. Sykes! Mr. Sy—" It was Sophie. She'd screamed. Scotty Sykes began pushing his thin weight against the wood panel.

But he did not have to try very long. Fargo opened the door, knife in hand, and said, showing brilliant teeth, "Greetings."

Scotty Sykes backed away. "What? What's—"

"Keep cool," Fargo said, "and you won't get hurt. —Too bad, Hedda. It almost worked."

"What the hell were you doing in there? Playing football?" Nobody answered her. She watched Cheeter drag Finley out in his chair. They'd put a gag in his mouth. A nylon stocking.

"Fin! Olga! What is this? What is this?" Scotty Sykes turned to Hedda. "And—and *you? You.*"

"That's right, *me.* Thought you had a piece of ass lined up, didn't you, motherfucker?"

"Cool it, Hedda," Fargo said. "Take him, Cheeter. Tie the sonofabitch up."

Scotty Sykes's face became as greasy as a slab of bacon. "Olga, what's this? Have they robbed you?"

Fargo undid Finley's gag and said, "Tell this cocksucker to keep quiet, and tell me where some more rope is."

"Good God, Fin! Good God! What in—"

"Don't fight it, Scotty," Finley said, working his jaw and sucking the insides of his cheeks. "Don't fight it. There's nothing you can do. They're both armed."

"You goddamn right," Fargo said, snapping his fingers. "Rope. Come on, rope."

"There isn't any more," Finley said.

"It better had be—for your buddy's sake. I mean like I don't want to have to stick this knife in his gut."

"In my room," said Sophie. She was massaging her left cheek. "Closet shelf. Left-hand side. Some wrapping cord."

Fargo pointed his knife at Cheeter. "Take him upstairs, Cheeter. Tie him up."

"To what?" Cheeter still had his sunglasses on.

"I don't give a shit. To anything. To the fucking bedpost."

"What are you going to do?" Scotty Sykes asked. "What are you going to do?"

"Come on," Cheeter said, pulling Scotty Sykes toward the stairs. "You want it rough or you want it easy?"

"But . . . but . . . Fin!"

Hedda followed Scotty Sykes and Cheeter to the stairway. In a voice that was light but rasping, the sound of rusty reeds, she shouted, "You no-good, bushwa, twopenny, fag-ass, slimy, rotten, freckled-face, motherfucker! You—you—" But she choked as she felt burning behind her eyes. She hated Scotty Sykes, but she hated worse having been forced to act the whore while Fargo stood behind the study door.

Fargo, taking his cue from habit, said, "Aw, good Jesus, Hedda, stop emotin'. You've got your Oscar for the season."

"What!" Hedda stormed down the foyer into the living room. "It was you bastards! You noisy sonsabitches! I'm out here doing my best and all I hear is bump-bump-bumpity-bump. Holy shit, it was worse than a pack of—"

"You enjoyed it," Fargo said, making himself a giant drink.

"I *enjoyed* it?"

"Yeah, yeah, you enjoyed it—so don't act so put out."

"You think I enjoyed acting like a slut? Making that bag of—"

"You'd enjoy making a telephone pole, baby, so don't hand me that."

"You're a lying shit. Fix me a drink."

"Fix it yourself."

As Hedda brushed past him to plunk two cubes into a glass, she saw the Blakes eyeing her. "Well," she said, tilting a great deal of gin, which she really didn't like, into her glass, "the pot oughtn't to call the kettle black, like they say. There're some mighty peculiar bones rattling around in *your* closet, doll. So I hear."

"What you mean?" Fargo snapped.

"Just what I said. You ain't such hot stuff."

"What you mean by that?"

"What I said. Just what I said, Fargo."

"You're full of shit."

"Yeah? Well, ask Cheeter. Ask Benny. You think nobody's onto your weirdo secret, dontcha, big shot? Huh? You needn't be putting me down and making me out to be a nympho 'cause I'll put your business in the street." Hedda whirled around, aware that the veins in her neck were throbbing. Throwing her hand into the air above her head, she snapped her fingers as she added, "Yes, I will."

That stopped him. He put down his drink. He slanted his eyes—an old trick, Hedda had seen it before—and said, "What about Benny? What about Cheeter? What kinda lie you mouthin', woman?"

"I know. I know."

"Know what?"

"What kind of freaky practices you been puttin' down." She sipped on her gin as though she enjoyed it, as if it were honey and nectar. "I know."

"Shee-ut," he said. "You don't know from nothin'."

"Wanna bet?"

"Then tell me. What did Benny say? What did Cheeter say?"

"What about me?" Cheeter said, coming down the stairs.

"He tied up?" Fargo asked.

"Yeah. What was you saying about—"

"Okay, back. Back out front."

"But I heard y'awl discussin' my name and I just—"

"Cheeter!" Fargo pointed a thumb toward the door, and Cheeter, shrugging his gorilla shoulders, went out. Fargo made whirlpools in his scotch with a long finger and then said, "So what did Cheeter say, huh?"

"I could tell you," Hedda said, suddenly buoyed up by Fargo's overreaction to something she'd thought to be only a rumor. Now she wondered. She really did wonder. "I could. But like my mama always use to say, 'The more you stir shit, the more it stinks.'" Her hand slid down her tomato-consommé dress, over her hipbone. She plucked at her thin thigh. "Right, Fargo? Right?"

Fargo didn't answer. There was only the sound of the wind outside getting tangled up in the trees. Finally, Sophie from the piano bench said in a voice starchy as Monday's washing, "Perhaps he—perhaps he doesn't want to stir, as it were. You suppose?"

"Quiet, Sophie," Finley said, squirming against the ropes at his waist. "Don't you mix in this."

But Sophie said, "Why not, Daddy? It is an awfully interesting metaphor, that, isn't it? About stirring, I mean. It's ever so much more vivid than that thing about letting sleeping dogs lie." She pinched her lips and then smiled an acid, girlish smile. "It might be entertaining, this stange practice Hedda seems to know about. What do you think, Fargo? What do you—"

"Cunt," he said quietly, walking slowly toward Sophie, "whyn't you turn you little foxy ass around on that bench and play me a tune?"

Sophie with her fists deep in her pockets said the wrong thing; she said, without batting an eye, "We've been through that bit before, it seems to me."

She'd barely finished speaking when Fargo, squinting his eyes, picked Sophie up and sat her at the piano, facing the keys. He took out his knife. He held it to her throat. "Not *this* way, we ain't. Play, cunt."

There were only a few seconds between Fargo's demand that Sophie play and Hedda's reaction, but to Hedda it seemed much longer. She fought down her jealousy, but Fargo's desire for Sophie with her coltish legs and her pinching lips was too obvious. With the special knowledge of her own love, Hedda saw what was taking place in spite of Fargo's rough words. Gin, and the need for revenge, went to her head, and she picked the nearest victim at hand—Finley. She'd already bent down and grabbed his crotch before she could calculate the effect it would have on Fargo.

"Good Lord, Miss Thing," she said softly to Olga, but loudly enough for Fargo to hear every syllable, "you're really doing all right for yourself, ain't you?"

Olga Blake rose. It was as if she didn't want to believe what she'd seen. Her voice shaking, she said, "Stop it! Stop it! Oh, make her stop it!" She walked haltingly toward Hedda, tears in her eyes.

Hedda flung out a talon hand, her eyes widening. "Sit your high-yellow ass back down."

"Fargo, I can't stand it, Fargo," Sophie said at the piano. "Please, Fargo. Please."

"Sit, bitch, sit. *Now* where's all your smart-ass talk? Huh? Play! Play the fucking piano!"

Olga came toward Hedda again, advanced in defense of Finley, who now sat with his legs clamped together, with his eyes closed, as if praying.

Hedda, with a searing swoop, slashed Olga across the cheek with her hand, her nails cutting into Olga's flesh and drawing blood. Olga recoiled from the flashing slap and even more from the contemptuous finger-wiping as Hedda smeared away a trickle of blood from her fingers upon Olga's dress. Fargo was shouting at Sophie, who had at last begun to play, "Faster, bitch! Faster! Faster!" Yet it was not a quartet of violence, but rather a duet, for it was really Hedda and Fargo who were coming to terms, perhaps disastrously, and Sophie and Olga were the least part of it.

(5)

IN THE kitchen, Olga applied a clean damp cloth to the cut on her cheek. The bleeding had stopped but there was a slight swelling around the area where Hedda's nails had torn her face. She wondered, outraged, if she would get lockjaw from it. Or rabies. After the fracas had died down, she'd asked to be allowed to go to her bedroom, where she could apply a medicated lotion to the wound, but Hedda vetoed that proposition flatly, declaring that cold water was good enough. Again, Olga pressed the cloth to her face. She looked at the clock above the refrigerator. It was nearly eleven, nearly sixty minutes before the midnight call, before . . . before—she did not know what.

Olga had not exactly reconciled herself to the no-exit situation with Fargo and Hedda, but at least she knew more or less what she could expect from them. The Committee was another matter. Sinister, unknown—the very idea of the Committee frightened her so much that the two alive and present in her living room seemed almost benign in comparison. At least she could see them, hate them. The stinging drained away from her cheek as she thought of the approaching midnight, and although she did not like the taste of it, she headed for the brandy in the living room. She decided to drink a lot of it, as much as she possibly could, to quiet the screaming of her nerves.

The brandy was not a small decision. Somewhere along the line, she'd come to feel that brandy was the proper thing to drink after dinner, the chic thing. Gin, she felt, was a low-class drink; she had heard in her childhood a Bessie Smith song that pleaded, "Gimme a pigfoot and a bottle of beer . . . a reefer and a gang of gin." The smoky, slightly acrid taste of scotch she could not stomach. Bourbon she shunned because (as Sybil Sykes had told her once over a vodka gibson on the rocks) bourbon was basically a Southern drink, and Olga had thrown away the South, the accent that went along with it, the memory of its humiliations. Liqueurs were too sticky. If the truth were known, it was Tab she most enjoyed, but that, of course, did not offer any anesthesia.

Before she could get the cork out of the brandy bottle, Finley said, "Careful, Olga. I'd take something lighter if I were you. Under stress, that 80 proof—"

"Under stress!" Olga whirled around. She attempted a bright, vindictive laugh but it sounded chunky, muffled, and realizing what a failure it had been, she poured twice as much brandy into the glass as she'd originally intended. "My husband says 'under stress.'" She stopped herself from extending her leg in a defiant stance as she'd seen Hedda do.

"But I know what I'm talking about, Olga," Finley said. "You don't drink in the first place and—and under conditions of stress, you——"

"Oh, for God's sake," she said, fighting an impulse to scream. "Shut up. Please, just shut up." She brought the glass of brandy to her nose. She didn't even like the smell of it. "Why not drink? Why not? A drunken corpse is better than a sober one. No, Fargo?"

Sophie chimed in. "But Daddy's right, Mother. You're already—"

"Oh, hush up, both of you." She took a swallow of the warm, cutting liquid and blinked. The strength of it made her eyes smart. "What do you think this is, anyway, a party?"

Someone had brought the card table from the study and placed it in the middle of the room. Fargo sat at the table, shuffling cards. He looked up and said, "Why not? Why not a party? You've got about an hour to make up your mind about that note. And me and Hedda's got an hour to wait for the Committee to call. I mean, loosen up—have a ball if you want. Do your thing." He cut the pack of cards and raised the deck in Finley's direction. Good-naturedly, yet with a note of derision, he said, "Wanna try a round?"

"No, no," Finley said, his hands free, smoking, but still bound by the ropes to the chair. "I don't have any heart for cards. I'm—I'm sorry. I just don't. It's a lifetime, it's a lifetime, Fargo, and you expect me to—"

"It's a lifetime, my ass." Fargo rolled the heel of his boot on top of the brown marble coffee table. "It's just $10,000—and Daddy, you've got the bread. That I know."

"What do you know?" Finley's cigarette ash fell to the rug. He stared at Fargo, through a curl of smoke wafting across his cheek, up past his graying hair. "What do you know about it? Do you think somebody sat down one day and *handed* this—all this to me? Do you suppose that? Oh no. Oh no, buddy, oh no! I burned midnight oil for years and years over one book after another. I wasn't one of these quick bright fellows, I had to work hard at it. I had to work hard at everything, as a matter of fact. Worked hard waiting tables. Driving taxis. Denied myself year after year after year. You know, Fargo, those weren't the days Harvard and Yale or wherever were snapping up Negro students as they do now. No, my friend. Far from it. There was no rush for black students then. I was damned lucky to get into Meharry —down in Nashville. And I almost didn't get in even there. Unh huh, nobody made it easy for *me*, Fargo. Nobody—all that hustling for tuition . . . cramming for exams . . . denying, denying almost everything— including a simple little thing like a cold bottle of beer . . . just *one* cold beer sometimes . . . including an ordinary thing like a dance once a month, or including once in a—"

"Including a piece of pussy every now and then?" Fargo threw his head back, smiled, slanted his eyes, and playfully rubbed his crotch as though it were a kitten's back.

"I married. I married Olga. And then *she* worked. She worked in offices and restaurants and cafeterias and in a plastic factory and in libraries and medical labs— and in all sorts of white kitchens and parlors. Oh no, oh no, my friend, nobody handed *us* anything. This house, those cars outside, my clinic—I mean, Christ, I haven't *always* had them, Fargo. They didn't just *happen*, Fargo. Don't you understand? You seem to think all this is some sort of luck from some sort of lottery ticket—as if, as if—Christ Almighty, one way or the other I've had to *fight* for it and *pay* for it. One way or the other. And you know, until fairly recently, too. As a matter of fact, just about—why, I think just about maybe twelve years ago, give or take a year, I once had to pay in a sort of way—I had to—we had to make a decision. I'd say, as a matter of fact, it was like paying through the nose. Worse than that. It was—it was in fact *the* supreme sacrifice—no less painful in its way than that man in the Bible with his—"

"Finley!" Olga put down her brandy. She'd heard, she'd heard! How dare he!

"What? I just said—I mean, I wasn't going . . . I wasn't going to say anything."

"You were, Finley Blake! You were! You'd let this man intimidate you into it. I know you would. Before you knew it, you'd've—"

"All right, Olga!" He threw away his cigarette and looked down at the ropes below his knees.

"You said, you'd never talk about it. You said *never*."

"I know I said I wouldn't, Olga. And I haven't. I—I didn't."

"What?" asked Sophie. "About what, Mother?"

"Nothing," Olga said. She drank her brandy as though it were Tab, and then choked on it.

"What decision, Daddy?" Sophie placed her hands flat upon the coffee table as if that gesture would prevent her parents' remarks from flying away. "What sacrifice? You said a decision."

"You bet he did," Hedda said. She was sitting at the card table across from Fargo, smoking. "And it sounded pretty high-flown to me." Hedda began a smile that drifted into a sneer. " 'A supreme sacrifice.' Shit, who do you think you are—Abraham or"—she leaned toward Fargo—"what was his name? That guy and the stone altar and all that crap they use to teach in Sunday school?"

Olga tried to crush her glass between her fingers, but it was a water glass. Her small fingers felt like bird claws around the warm hard crystal. She stared at Hedda. Her ears burned. Her throat burned. "You—you morbid, morbid—"

"Pick up, Mrs. Bitch, don't morbid me none—it was your husband who first said something about that sacrificing bit. Remember? Not me."

"Daddy—Daddy, for crying out loud, what is it? What were you talking about?"

Finley, his head lowered, looking down at the rug, said, "Nothing, love. Your mother—your mother gets a bit hysterical on liquor and starts into things that ought to be left—"

"*I? I?* You rotten bastard, you rotten bastard, you rotten bastard!"

"Now," Hedda said to Finley, to egg Olga on, "how about *them* apples?"

Olga drained her glass and threw it into the magazine rack. It didn't break. It stuck, in between *House & Garden* and *Twenty-One Easy Sweaters*. She held her stomach and bent slightly forward. "O God in heaven. O God in heaven. Do you think I ever forget? Ever? Ever? And you—you, God, I didn't bring it up, I didn't. I try to forget but you think I ever forget? You rotten bastard. Ever? I said 'yes' for you—not for *me,* Finley Blake. It didn't matter to me if you ended up doing General Practice instead of going on and on and on— I didn't want to, God knows, I didn't want to."

Finley kept his eyes closed tightly, as though he thought it would help shut off the sound of Olga's voice.

"Never, never, did I want to, Finley Blake, but when I told you that day—oh, when I told you that afternoon in that rundown smelly—smelly—yes! Yes! Fargo, young man, we've been poor, too—*poor, poor, poor.* We haven't always lived at the castle. And *arrogance?* I've never seen arrogance until you came here tonight with your black revolution this and your black revolution that, with your knife and with your gun and with your Afro hair and with your gold earring. What—tell me, what do *you* know about drinking fountains marked 'white' and drinking fountains marked 'colored' and being called 'auntie' and being called 'girl' by twerpy saleswomen and being called—called worse and seeing— seeing—young man, I've seen worse than rats, but I don't go around trying to crash the world down over my head because somebody makes misery for some- body else.

"And *rats? Rats?* Is that the worst you've seen? Is it? Have you seen—God in heaven, in Anniston, Alabama, one day! Have you ever seen a pregnant woman get beat in the belly with a monkey wrench by a pecker- wood bus driver? And only because she was sitting with her husband—who was dark and—and—she looked too white to be colored? *Rats?* Is that all that makes your wrath come up and blow your prettified Afro head? *Is it?*

"Oh, Fargo, Fargo . . . in my way, in my way, I've been fighting forty years to get *you* where *you* are now, and then you turn on me, on us, just because we want to get some goodness out of this rotten life before—before—and I've paid for it, I've paid for it, and not by just seeing rats and plaster falling.

"Call it white, call it whitey's way, call it what you want, but I want it, you understand? Don't make any mistake about it, because I want it and I want it now. And—and *bourgeois?* Bourgeois, indeed. Where did you pick up that little clever, half-cooked-up, tricky idea anyway? Sounds like a piece of something left over from the Russian Revolution. Do you even know what it means? Do you? Bah, I swear, I swear, give you a bank account and a car and you'd out-bourgeois any-body on this street. Anybody, anybody on this street. Do you hear me? You—you mixed-up hoodlum!"

Fargo glanced over his shoulder, as though looking for an eavesdropper. Then he turned back to Olga with raised chin and squinting eyes.

"You know, I know you for what you are—what you really are beneath that—that costume and those—those bully-boy ways of yours. I do, I do, Fargo, I do! Take my money. Take my life, but let me call the cards by their right names. Oh God! God!"

She hadn't realized it until they were in her hand, but she'd picked up the deck of cards from the table. She looked at them through the tears blurring her lashes and then slung them across the living-room floor, the jack of clubs falling on Finley's lap, diamonds and spades sliding across the stones of the hearth.

"*Ho*-ly shit," Hedda said and rose to make herself a drink.

It was quiet in the room. Olga could hear the wind running in and out of the plastic umbrella trimmings.

Then Sophie said, questioning, her eyes probing the past, "I ought to know. I ought to know what happened. On 117th Street, Mother?"

"You know."

"What do you mean, I know? I was—I was five. At least. Wasn't I? Well, *wasn't* I?"

"You know."

"Mother, you're drunk. You say I know and I don't. Daddy . . . Daddy?"

'A chamber pot, Sophie, is a chamber pot," Olga said. "A cham—"

"A Vorteck Sanitary Disposal," Finley cut in harshly.

"A chamber pot, Finley! A chamber pot . . . a . . . my . . . oh God, what time is it?" Olga looked over to the clock by the staircase, but the hands were blurred. They seemed to be wavering. "What time—oh, what does it matter? Vorteck. What does it matter—it was a chamber pot to Sophie. Wasn't it, Sophie? It was a chamber pot to you, wasn't it?"

Sophie looked away from Olga and said, "Mother, if you're drunk, just shut up."

"Yes. Yes, even my own daughter tells me to shut up—don't you, daughter, dear? A chamber pot, you thought it was. Didn't you?"

"Sophie was—was five. Come on. We agreed, Olga." Finley pulled against the ropes at his waist. "Remember? You agreed as well as—"

"I do, I do, Finley. Right on that table—oh God, right on that round kitchen table on 117th Street you gouged and gouged all that new life in me. I'll always remember that scraping—that was the worst part, that scraping and scraping and that pain and that dirty rosebud wallpaper and that roach running out of the toaster to watch you scraping, waiting it was, and watching you scrape and scrape . . . and then that awful chamber pot. . . ."

"I told you before, Olga . . . I got it from the lab. . . . It . . ."

"Well, it might as well've been a chamber pot, for all I know—for all she knew. She—she saw you. She saw you. I've always known that. Always."

Hedda swirled ice cubes around in her glass and winked at Sophie maliciously. "Did you really see your daddy chuck your baby brother into a chamber pot?"

"Cut it out!" Finley shouted. He kicked against the ropes binding his feet. "Now, cut it out. It was, after all, only a fetus. It wasn't a brother. It was—it was— so I had to do an abortion. So what's so wrong with that, anyway? Olga, you agreed—you—we agreed."

Sophie stood, and said, as though she were spelling the words out in her mind, "Chamber pot."

Olga picked up a melting ice cube she'd dropped, or somebody had dropped, from the rug. She stared at the cube melting in the palm of her hand. "She saw. I know." She sat on the piano bench, with her hand stretched out over her lap, staring at the cube melting in her palm, trying to feel the pain of the icy melting, provoking pain to test her control over it, but she could not feel the pain of it; the cube was cold and melting and numbing the center of her hand but she could not, even as she concentrated, feel the pain of the melting of it.

"I've remembered," she told Finley. "I've always re- membered. On the stairs . . . her pigtails between the balustrades, those filthy balustrades in the hall, and her eyes staring at me flat upon that kitchen table.

" 'Sophie, Sophie . . . run along and play . . . run out and play' . . . but Sophie sat on the hallway stairs, like somebody's stranger, not like our child, while you washed off the instruments . . . your prongs and scrapers stained dark with the blood of the child we couldn't afford to have."

Olga watched the puddle in her palm grow, and she talked carefully so as not to make ripples in it, so as not to disturb it.

"But Sophie came," she said, her eyes steady on the puddle in her hand, "She did—oh, yes, she came, all right—straight in the kitchen to that chamber pot at the end of the table. I couldn't move . . . half dead, half . . . I couldn't stop her from . . . looking at it . . . my five-year-old baby from looking at it . . . pulling off that lid of that chamber pot that afternoon in that kitchen."

She turned to Sophie. "It was after, after that, Sophie, it was after that you never came to our bed with the funnies anymore. It was after that . . ."

Sophie rubbed her elbows and slowly shook her head.

"It was after that, Sophie."

"I don't think I want him anymore," she said.

"It was soon after that." The ice in Olga's hand had now melted but the puddle was still there. "After that you never came—"

"I don't want him, I don't want him."

"And I'll always remember her eyes. Her bright eyes. Looking through that balustrade. Looking at me on that table. . . . God, how can I not remember that?"

"I don't—I just don't remem—"

"Oh yes, oh yes, young lady, oh yes."

Sophie shook her head again, in slow motion, with a frown at her lips.

"I know very well you've remembered that." Olga began speaking faster. Words broke away from her like whiplashes. "And a million ways you've never let me forget it, either, Sophie. Have you, Sophie. Have you?"

Sophie was standing over Teddy, her head bent down toward him, but she did not seem to be looking at him. She whispered when she said, "I don't want Teddy anymore."

The puddle of water in Olga's hand had become warm. The puddle moved. It rolled across her palm to her thumb. It spilled on top of the glossy piano bench.

"Why don't you keep him, Mother?" Sophie asked, without taking her vacant stare away from the bear. Her voice, however, had become hard, alert. "Here," she said as she picked him up and dropped him in Olga's lap. "He's yours now."

Olga jumped up and Teddy fell to the floor. "What do you mean by that, Sophie? What do you mean by that?"

Sophie put her fists into her pockets and looked steadily into Olga's eyes. "He's yours now, Mother." She then nudged Teddy in the back with her sneaker but kept her eyes locked to Olga's. "What's the matter? Don't you want him?" Sophie then gently pushed the bear across Olga's foot and said, "Mother?"

Olga saw yellow goldfish from the lamplight swim across Sophie's round steel-rimmed glasses. She couldn't see Sophie's eyes. She could only see the swimming yellow goldfish. She became afraid, afraid of her own daughter. She picked up Teddy and beat him softly about the shoulders, and hugged him, and beat him softly again, both in love for the animal and in fear of the animal.

Then she sat back down on the piano bench with the bear in her arms. Teddy, Teddy. It had been twelve years ago, nearly thirteen, when she'd bought the bear in some frantic and heartbroken attempt to make amends for the carelessness of leaving the kitchen door unlocked—where Sophie had seen, Sophie had watched. Even at the time, Olga knew it was foolish—but it wasn't as though she'd deliberately gone out to hunt for the bear. It wasn't as though it had been coldly calculated. It had just happened. When she saw it, there in Schwarz's window, she bought it on the spot, feeling that the larger the compensation, the sooner she might see forgiveness in Sophie's eyes.

"Now, if I may," Sophie said, half to Finley, half to nobody in particular, hiking up her round glasses closer to her face, "I'm going to have a small drink."

Everyone watched Sophie make her drink. If there is one line—one small moment in time—that divides a girl from womanhood, Sophie had just passed it, crossed over. She was still Sophie, but more Sophie than before. No one spoke. Everyone watched her as she sat and raised the glass to her lips. It seemed as though she were making a toast to herself, as if she were having a private celebration. Just as she took her first sip, the telephone rang.

At the same moment Cheeter opened the front door and stared at the phone.

"Hello," Fargo said. "Hello? Who? Naw, ain't nobody here by that name. You got the wrong number."

"Who was it?" Cheeter asked.

"Some joker. Wrong number."

"Are you sure it was a wrong number?" Finley leaned forward in his chair. "Who did they ask for?"

"Man, I know a wrong number when I hear it. Some cat with a big thick accent. Spanish maybe."

"He write that note yet?" Cheeter asked. The collar of his old-fashioned suit was pulled up to the curve of his black turtleneck sweater.

"Not yet."

"Well, shit, Fargo, what you waitin' for?"

"What do you mean?"

"Well, *make* him write the fuckin' note, man. What you been doing all this time?"

"Listen, Cheeter, the Committee don't pay you to think—they pay you for your goddamn muscle. If you'd—"

"Hedda," Cheeter said, turning away from Fargo, "what in the fuck's going on?" He took off his sunglasses, and then, as if the lamplight were too strong for his eyes, he stuck them quickly back on. "I thought you and Fargo was going to get him to sign that note thing."

Hedda didn't bother to look up from her cards. She had taken the second deck and was playing solitaire. "You know what your job is," she said. "Do it. Leave us alone."

"Right," Fargo said. "Now, get the hell outside and watch."

Cheeter started to leave, then stopped. He turned, rubbing his arms. "Well, gimme a little taste. Y'awl been having a ball in here while I been—"

"A ball? A ball?" Olga stood up. Teddy fell to the floor. She stumbled as she went over to Cheeter. "Oh, but you do have a divine sense of humor," she said. "Yes, yes, a ball. Do come in and join us." She held onto the banister curve in the foyer for support. She had never been drunk before and she was surprised that her feet felt numb.

Fargo fanned the air with his big hand as if he were shooing pigeons. "Get going, Cheeter, get going."

"Well, gimme a taste first. It's cold out there and—"

"Here, damn it," Fargo said, grabbing a half bottle of Johnnie Walker. "Take the fucking bottle with you and git."

"Jeez, Johnnie Walker!" Cheeter said, inspecting the amount of scotch in the bottle as well as the label. "Y'awl been living it—"

"Out! You hear me?"

When Cheeter closed the door, Olga spoke in a voice she intended to be crisp, but it came in wet slurs, with a hint of Southern accent. "He does," she said, "have— have good taste in alcoholic beverages, I gather, doesn't he? I mean, for a hoodlum. As for myself," she said, on the way to the liquor cabinet, "I'll have another fat splash of brandy."

Finley reached out from his chair and tried to stop her, but she dodged him. "You'll be very sick, Olga. Drunk. In fact, you're already on the—"

"Why not?" she asked. "For God's sake, why not? You expect me to sit around and watch a bunch of thugs slowly tease and destroy us? Bit by bit? I rather be drunk when they shoot us than sober." She poured brandy. "So why not? *You* certainly aren't doing anything to stop all this. 'No, Olga.' 'No, Sophie.' All this dillydallying. If you had any sort of gumption, you'd— you'd—"

"I'd what?" Finley asked.

"Oh, I don't know," she said, putting the brandy down without drinking it.

"That was vicious and unfair, Mother, and you know it." Sophie got up from the bay window and put her empty glass down on the cabinet next to Olga's brandy. "What is he supposed to do—tied up like that in that—"

"Oh, go play your Mozart."

"Let Teddy, Mother. Let Teddy."

Olga's hand was already on the downswing, past

Sophie's chin, before she realized she'd slapped her.
Sophie turned and said, "Don't you . . . don't you
ever. Hit. Me. Again. Ever."

"There isn't going to be any ever again. They're
going to kill us. Aren't you? Aren't you, Fargo?"

"You hit me, Mother. You've always wanted to do
that—haven't you?"

"And why *don't* you kill us and get it over with?"
Olga steadied her gaze upon Fargo's black satin face.
"Afraid the neighbors'll hear the pistol shots? Afraid
they'll come running?"

"You've wanted to hit me since that day, haven't
you? Haven't you? Answer me!"

"No, not these neighbors," Olga went on, almost
falling as she swirled her arm around in the direction
of all her neighbors. "Not *these* neighbors. These
neighbors—"

"Haven't you?" Sophie asked. "Haven't you?"

"Yes! Yes! I . . . no, no . . . I . . ." Olga looked
down at her hand, the hand that had hit Sophie. The
room darkened. She felt she must lie down. The numb-
ness of her feet began rising to her knees. She fought
a wave of nausea. She headed for the kitchen. But the
nausea passed. She lay upon a caned-back settee near
the study. Before she closed her eyes, the figures in the
room—Fargo, Hedda, Teddy, Finley, Sophie—looked
like underwater dancers. With eyes. Glass eyes. Watching her.

"DARLINGS, I must tell you the most heaven bit of—oh, I *am* sorry. I had no idea you were having a . . ."

It was Sybil Sykes, standing in the foyer, her platinum laughter corroding to rusty iron as she looked around the room. Hedda was more startled at the woman's resemblance to her husband up in the bedroom—even to the freckles—than she was to see her standing there near the front door. There was no sign of Cheeter.

"Finley," the woman said, coming down into the living room, "what sort of—good heavens, what sort of silly game are you—where's Scotty?"

It had been so sudden, Sybil's giddy entrance into the house, that neither Hedda nor Fargo had time to rise from the card table. They had forgotten to bolt the door when Cheeter left with the half bottle of scotch, and the woman had just walked right in.

"And Olga?" Sybil Sykes said. "Is Olga . . . ?" She turned to look at Olga, still curled up on the caned-back settee. "What, for God's sake, is going on here, Finley?"

Hedda stared at Sybil. She was still stunned by the woman's resemblance to Scotty Sykes. They looked like brother and sister. Twins, even. Her freckles, Hedda could see now, were ruddier than Scotty's, and she did not have as many as Scotty had, but nearly everything else looked the same. While Sybil stood in the middle of the living room sputtering, demanding information from Finley, and gasping at his answers, Hedda began to put price tags on Sybil's orange pants suit, her peach square-toed shoes, the dangling row of Indian bracelets on her wrist, the green, slippery-looking earrings. She knew the type—a woman with money who had nothing to do all day but hunt for the latest fashions in Manhattan's expensive stores.

Sybil flung her arms about (as if for no other reason than to clank her Indian bracelets) and stammered, "*Ten* thousand dollars—*here*, in St. Albans?" Hedda decided that Sybil, too, smelled of peppermint and lime.

"And what's so special about St. Albans?" Fargo asked, his knife blade poking in the air as he started to the front door.

"Oh, God. Oh, God." Sybil laughed quickly and fingered the thin bracelets at her wrist. "Excuse me, but it's—it's—it always happens somewhere else. I mean, *here?*"

As much as Hedda detested and resented Sybil, she

could not deny a creeping admiration for the woman's control, her cool. "Yeah, *here,*" she said. "Is St. Albans so special, honey?"

Sybil looked at Hedda for the first time. Her hands went up to puff around the swirls of her frizzled hair. "I beg your pardon," Sybil said, lifting her eyebrows to reveal a hint of green eyeshadow. "I am not 'honey.' Sybil Sykes." As she dropped her hands and raised her chin, she asked, "And you?"

"Miss Brewster, honey, Miss Brewster."

"Why you insufferable little—"

"Easy, Sybil," Finley said. "This is no game. This is—"

"Well, I should hope not," Sybil said, "but the appalling incivility of—"

"Aw, shut up, bitch," Fargo said, as he came back from the door. "I've had enough of your lip. Where in the fuck is Cheeter? How'd you get in here?" He came closer to Sybil, inspecting her peach shoes, her frizzled curls. "Didn't you see a—a cat out there with a—a—"

"With a bottle? Sitting in Finley's car?" She laughed and clanged her bracelets. "Had I known . . . had I but *known!* Silly of me, really."

Hedda snorted. The woman's assurance angered her, not only because it smacked of a kind of put-down (like Scotty Sykes), but also because Hedda found, against her will, she admired it; it had style.

"And speaking of drinking," Sybil said, "I think *I'll* have a bit of something. A tiny cognac." She headed toward the liquor cabinet before anybody could speak. "You don't mind, do you? Oh, and *do* put away that ugly instrument," she said, her long slinky arm dipping for a second in the direction of Fargo's switchblade. "It's really quite too much," and, pouring herself a drink, she added, "and totally unnecessary. Are you afraid of us? Three women and a man bound up?" She came back, smiling. Her teeth were stained from too many cigarettes. "Incidentally," she said to Fargo, "I didn't catch your name. I'm Sybil Sykes."

Fargo paused on the two steps leading to the foyer. "Fargo, if you want to know."

"Fargo? Fargo? Hmmm, you mean like the truck people? Fargo Wells? Or is it Wells Fargo? I do get them crossed up. Sometimes I think I—" But Fargo was at the front door shouting for Cheeter.

Sybil, with her cognac, sat on the sofa. "Come, Sophie, love, sit with me. Tell me your news. I haven't talked to you in ages."

Sophie sat down on the sofa, her fists in her pockets. "There's no news to tell. Except what you can see!"

Hedda wagged her head with insolent grace and rolled her tongue across her teeth.

"But Bennington, dear. Aren't you thrilled?" Sybil continued.

"I don't go for another two weeks," Sophie said.

Finley shot a glance at the clock, as if he expected it to be a calendar.

"But aren't you thrilled? About the prospect and everything? I mean Maggie Coleman's little girl over on Woodlawn was—oh, I shouldn't say 'little girl' anymore, should I? It's dreadfully difficult to remember you aren't anybody's little girls anymore. But you know Patsy, don't you? Maggie Coleman's girl? She must be about your—"

"Can't find him." Fargo came back inside and closed the door. "Wait till I get my hands on that no-good motherfucker."

"Mr. Fargo," Sybil said, her voice sounding as if it were sailing across rooftops, "that is a *fright*ful expression. Must you use it in front of ladies?"

"Up your giggie, girlie." Fargo paced the floor for a bit, ignoring Sybil and looking at his watch. Then he put his knife in his pocket and walked over to the card table. "Come on, Hedda. Let's try another hand. Cut."

"I did." Hedda was watching Sybil's arms. They flew around like ship flags.

"Any cigarettes, love?" Sybil asked Finley.

"There're some in that little box," Finley said, "by the lamp. And bring me one."

Sybil lit Finley's cigarette for him and turned to Sophie. "You, dear?"

"No. No, thank you."

"And throw me that journal, would you, Sybil?"

Finley pointed to the magazine rack. "No, no—next to that thing on knitting. No, back. Right."

Olga, who had seemed dead to the world, rolled off the settee and stumbled out of the room and into the kitchen. She was audibly sick.

"Good heavens," Sybil said, putting down her cigarette. As she started toward the kitchen, Hedda said, "Where do you think you're going?"

"In—in—she's sick. Can't you hear it?"

Hedda said, "Sit."

"But she's—she's—" Sybil continued toward the kitchen.

"Sit, I said!" Hedda rose, longing to hit her. She was almost sorry when Sybil obeyed.

Hedda picked up her cards and said as if to herself: *"What an evening—this evening with the Blakes."* But the words were not as acid on her tongue as she'd planned them, and her hands were trembling with hate. First of all, the orange pants suit cost as much as Hedda's rent for three months. Maybe four months. And she knew Sybil Sykes had spent the better part of the day driving into town, sitting under the dryer, getting her frizzles frizzled. At a moment like this, Hedda could believe all those words Fargo had poured out, all the preaching he'd done. The bushwa bastards deserved to be fleeced! All of them.

But it was also at a moment like this that Hedda was most evasive about and to herself. Although she was normally honest—or tried to be—she could not allow one bitter truth: she was there because of Fargo and only because of Fargo. In theory, she could go along with his talk of revolution, or even just plain car-stealing, but she could not admit that she probably would also go along with Fargo if he were merely repairing tents for Boy Scouts. This buried knowledge smoldered and turned into an unnamed anger, which, like acid, ate away at her self-esteem.

"Hit me," Fargo said. They were playing Black Jack. Hedda tried to concentrate on the game.

"Shit," Fargo said, not pleased with his luck.

"I suppose," Sybil was saying to Sophie, "it's just as well, what with cancer and emphysema and God knows what else—I mean, I'm not exactly advocating it, you know, your smoking, but there is a certain style, you know, the whole ritual of it, and Bennington is a terribly sophisticated place, I understand. I mean, I'm not saying you ought to smoke, but there are certain styles, my dear, that—well, Sophie, you *have* been sheltered, you know. You really ought to—ah, but what am I saying?"

Sybil laughed deprecatingly and jangled her bracelets. "And *that* . . . darling, you mustn't take *that*. Teddy, I mean. I trust you aren't. It's really very neurotic, your Teddy. Not Teddy itself, of course, but—but—on more than one occasion I've said to Olga, I've

said, 'Olga, darling, there's something positively un-
natural between Teddy and Sophie.' You know what
I mean? It's not just the size, darling, that's so—so—
off-putting . . . in fact, that's rather fun . . . but,
honestly, it's—it's, well, quite frankly, and I *might* be
wrong, but I've always had the *faintest* suspicion that
you really don't like Teddy at all. You know?"

Although Hedda was listening to Sybil Sykes and
fuming inwardly at her peppermint-lime cologne, she
didn't miss seeing Fargo's fingers cautiously extended.
"That's not your card, Fargo."

"Sorry."

"I bet."

"But as I was saying . . . what was I saying?" Sybil
continued. "Oh yes, Patsy. That Coleman girl. Patsy
Coleman, you know her? Her father owns those stucco
apartment buildings over on Linden Boulevard. But
poor darling, she's not as lucky as you, I must say. No
Bennington for her. *Nor* Smith. *Nor* Bryn Mawr. *Nor*
Vassar. And it's not, my dear, as if they were still dis-
criminating against Negroes these days. You know, she
just simply isn't bright enough, Patsy isn't. As a matter
of fact, let's face it: she's a dumb little fat thing, poor
darling, when you get right down to it.

"And her mother—and really, as though I couldn't
see through that—she said, Maggie said, 'I really think
it's best to expose Patsy to her own crowd—to Negro

boys she might marry.' Maggie meant Howard, of
course. Or Tuskegee. Or Hampton. Or someplace like
that. Imagine!"

Sybil lit another cigarette. "Well . . . now, *you*.
What about you? I mean, are there boys there in Bennington? I heard it's an all-girls school, am I right? Yes,
I'm sure. Pity, too, isn't it? About dates, I mean. I
mean, where there's no smoke there's no fire—or is it
the other way around? Well, you know what I mean.
Sophie?"

"Yes?"

Sybil made a quick survey about the room, her eyes
secretly studying Fargo and Hedda at the card table.
She said, "Tell me, does Olga—does your mother still
have that astrology calendar in the kitchen? Up near
the spice rack?"

"Yes—yes, I think so. It's funny. I see it so much
I *don't* see it. You get so used to—but I'm sure it's still
there. Why?"

"And you have some scouring things? Powder and
stuff?"

"Of course. I mean, I don't exactly know what, or
how much, but certainly there must be *some*. What's—"

"So the calendar is still there. And there's scouring
powder."

"Yes. Sure. What's the—sure, why?"

"And you still play, of course. Your piano pieces.
Have you been working on anything recently?"

"Yes. No. I pick at a lot of things. I sometimes—"

"Oh, do you?"

"Yes. Yes, Mrs. Sykes. But I'm really not in the mood to—"

"Thank you, thank you, sir," Hedda said, scooping up a trick from Fargo. "You sure you don't want to play for money, honey?"

"I see!" Sybil continued firmly. "Now. You have the calendar still, and there's—"

"Of course, of course, but I don't—"

"Listen. Just listen, darling. Again, you have the zodiac thing—the calendar. Near the *spice rack*, no?"

"I said I think so. There's that calendar, and the spice rack, right next to the tele—"

"Of course, you do play still, don't you? You understand, don't you? Things with lots of brio and fortissimo and—"

Fargo threw them an irritated look.

"Your play," Hedda said.

"Do you mean—" Sophie said.

"I mean that I'd love to hear something, you know, right now. With fire to it. While I'm in the kitchen— you know, cleaning poor Olga's sick mess. Do you follow? I mean, no Debussy, or Mozart, or—"

"Rachmaninoff?"

"With lots of fortissimo, perhaps?"

"The C-sharp minor Prelude? I can finger through it."

"*Molto bene,* darling."

"Shall I start now? Right away?"

"It's clear, then?"

"Oh yes. Very."

"Jesus!" Fargo clucked his tongue. "It's a good thing I ain't playing for no money."

"Tough titty." Hedda glanced at the cards in her hand. "And what was that you just put down? Eight of diamonds, wasn't it?"

"Eight of diamonds."

"Hmmm . . . huh, I thank you again."

"Shit."

"Shall I play now, Sybil? The Prelude?"

"Just a second or two, dear." Sybil rose, flinging her arms as if she were rearranging the air about her. She went to the card table. "My, my," she said, smiling with her stained teeth, "you two are really at it, aren't you? Who's winning?"

"Me," Hedda said, forgetting for a moment her enemy; she was basking in her luck.

Sybil Sykes leaned over the table and said, "You know, I've always wanted to play cards well. I'm awful at it, really. Guilt, I guess. From my Baptist background. A sense of sin and all that, I suppose. I mean, once I got away from home I learned to drink and I learned to smoke, but, alas, I never could get on with cards very well." She laughed in gay skips. Her hand flounced up to touch her collarbone. "Life is funny, isn't it? I mean, the petty sins are the ones that really enslave us, I think. D'you agree?"

Hedda shot a glance at Fargo. "Sounds like we got a philosopher in the crowd tonight."

"Oh, *you*," Sybil said with a husky giggle. "Tell me, what are these cards? I mean, why are they all of the same—"

"Hush, bitch! You wanna give my hand away?"

"Sorry. I was only curious about—"

"Well, be curious about Fargo's hand if you gotta be curious."

"I was just—just . . . Terribly sorry." She walked around the card table and then said suddenly, brightly, "Maybe I'll—shall I play something? On the piano?"

"Play if you want," Fargo said, not looking up from his hand. "*That* one over there don't do nothing but pick around."

Sybil laughed again, her flinging arms conducting her laughter. "Ho-ho, now I know better than that. Don't I know better than that, Sophie? I've heard you dozens of times. Why don't you show them? Why don't you play something? Hmm, Sophie?"

When Sophie got up and went to the piano, Sybil said, "Good, good. Our dear Sophie, ladies and gentlemen, is going to give us a little recital. Meanwhile—meanwhile, I suppose, meanwhile I should help out Olga. I mean, since I blundered in here like this, I suppose I should make myself useful." On the way to the kitchen, she bubbled, "Play, darling. Play so I can hear you."

Fargo stood up, his mind off the cards at last. "Hold it. Where you going?"

"To tidy up a bit. You have no idea how sour it'll smell if that—if *that* isn't cleaned up. The stench will permeate the entire place. And I'll bring out some more ice, too, shall I? Play, darling, play."

Olga shifted her position on the settee and mumbled something that sounded like "Oh, Sybil, don't bother," but Sophie had already begun to play.

"What's got into *her?*" Fargo asked Hedda.

"Inspiration, I expect—but it's giving me a head-ache."

"Is that kitchen door locked?" Fargo asked.

"What?"

"The kitchen door, Hedda! It's locked, no?"

"Yes, yes. I told you once before. Deal." She waited for him to distribute the cards. She'd never played cards with Fargo before. She was surprised how much pleasure it gave her to beat him: her ears were humming from the sudden rush of blood to her head.

But Fargo did not continue to deal. His eyes darted to the telephone. He dropped the cards and went over to the phone. He grabbed it from its cradle. He listened and then bolted for the kitchen.

"Making a little phone call, huh, baby?" Fargo

pushed Sybil into the living room by the seat of her pants suit.

"Get your filthy hands off me!" she ordered.

"Huh? A little phone call, huh?"

Sybil's freckles turned darker.

"Get Cheeter, Hedda. Find the fucker."

But Cheeter, made uneasy by the volume of music coming from the house, was already at the front door. "What's up?" he asked, and seeing Sybil, he added, "Who's that?"

"Yeah," Fargo sneered, " 'who's that?' You should ask, you no-good sonofabitch. She walked straight on in from the front door, man. It could've been a whole fucking army."

"I was—"

"You were out in the car boozing," Hedda said.

"Who is this broad, anyway?" Cheeter said.

"Weren't you?" Hedda insisted.

"Weren't I what? Gettin' me a taste?"

"Will you please take your sweaty paws off me?" One of Sybil's bracelets had fallen to the floor.

"Bring down some rope," Fargo said. "I'm gonna tie this bitch up, too. No—wait." A white smile broke across his face. "Take her up and tie her up next to her old man."

"What are you going to do, Fargo?" Finley on the other side of the room, across from the sofa, seemed to be left out. "There's no need to—no need—Sybil won't be of any—"

"That *is* your old man upstairs, ain't it?" Fargo said. "That freckled-faced freak we tied to the bedpost?"

"Fargo?" Finley said.

Sybil ripped her arm out of Cheeter's grasp. "You needn't pull at my flesh and bones like that. I'll walk up, thank you. I shan't fly away. Do you understand?"

Cheeter didn't seem to know just what to do. "Okay," he said. "Go up 'head."

Hedda lit a cigarette and waved her hand at Sybil. "Beddy-bye, honey."

Sybil Sykes turned and looked down the stairs. "Mrs. Sykes to you, my dear. Mrs. Sykes."

"Mrs. Sykes, your mama," Hedda said, but realized, almost as soon as she said it, the woman would not understand the insult of Playing the Dozens.

During the commotion, Olga had come back to life and now sat on the edge of the settee, but she still seemed half asleep, drugged. She walked unsteadily across the room as if she were trying to avoid potholes in the rug. They all watched her, wondering if she was heading for the brandy again, but she stopped and sat primly upon the piano bench.

In a very short time, Cheeter came back down the steps. "Now what?" he asked.

"You finished, already?" Fargo shot a glance up the

staircase. "That was mighty quick. You tie the bitch up good and tight?"

"She ain't getting out of them ropes."

"Where'd you put her?"

"Like you said, Fargo. Next to her old man. To the bedpost."

"Okay, go. Now stay out there in *front* of the house, goddamn it. I mean it, now."

When Cheeter left, Finley said, "Okay, untie me, Fargo. I can't sign anything tied up like this. All right?"

Instead of replying, Fargo stood there in an odd day-dream staring at Sophie's knees and at the blue denim skirt covering her thighs. "What?" he said, snapping out of it. "Yeah, you've decided you're gonna—just a minute," he said, starting up the stairs. "Lemme go check on those motherfuckers. I can't trust Cheeter no further'n I can see."

Nobody spoke as they waited for Fargo to return. Hedda listened to the wind whining around the house and to Cheeter's clumsy feet tromping over twigs and dried leaves. The room smelled like a barroom. And Olga's vomit smelled like vomit.

When Fargo came back downstairs, Finley said, "Are you going to untie me, Fargo? So I can sign?"

"You hands are free, man. You don't write with your feet."

Finley shook his head. "It's the indignity of it. Fargo,

it's the indignity of it. Come on, come on, for God's
sake."

Fargo hesitated, then he said, "Aw, what the fuck."
As soon as he got the first of the ropes undone, the ropes
loose from Finley's arms, Finley began: he grabbed the
earring at Fargo's ear and pulled in an attempt to slice
the gold hook through the earlobe.

Finley and Fargo fell to the floor.

Fargo was torn between trying to pry Finley's hand
away from the ring in his ear and at the same time
fishing for his gun. His hands went up and down, back
and forth, as he tried to get the gun out of the holster
and to keep his ear from being torn apart. It had happened so fast, and Finley's chair had tipped over in
such a way, that Hedda could find no place to come to
Fargo's aid. By the time she could get into the fight,
Fargo had pulled away from Finley and now had his
knife in his hand.

"Back!" Fargo snarled. "Back, motherfucker! Back!"

Fargo lay on the floor next to Finley. They were no
more than inches apart. The only thing between them
was the switchblade knife.

(7)

FARGO TOUCHED his ear. There was a thin cut on the lobe. A bit of blood. The frail hook had been dime-store stuff; it had broken. It had not, as Fargo felt it had and Finley hoped, ripped through the flesh of his ear. But then, as if the pain and humiliation were not enough, Cheeter showed up at the door to put his five cents in. "Man, can't you handle these folks?" he said, looking at Finley strapped to his chair on the floor.

Fargo spit back, "Why in the hell aren't you around when we need you?"

Cheeter waved his scotch bottle in a circle, benignly. "I'm 'round. I been 'round. What's up this time?"

"Nothing *now*, you motherfucker. I'm gonna report your ass. You hear?"

"Why, man? Why? You told me to stay outside, didn't you? When I heard all that fuss y'awl was making, I came. Didn't I? Ain't my fault you can't handle this scene, Fargo. Ain't my—"

"Get out!"

"Well, don't be puttin' no bad mouth on me, just because you—"

"Get out, goddamn it, get out!" Fargo leaped up the two steps to the foyer and gave Cheeter and his bottle a shove. He slammed the door. The ornaments on the mantel rattled. "Tilt him right side up, Hedda. Tie the bastard's arms up again."

"Don't you be hollering and shouting at me," Hedda snapped as she pulled Finley up and started tying his arms. "I'm not just another flunky . . . all this hassle for—"

"Do I need crap from you, too?"

"Crap? All I said was—"

"I don't wanna hear no more. Understand? Just don't speak. Okay?"

Hedda stopped yanking at the ropes around Finley's arms and glared at Fargo. "Listen, baby, now you just listen to me. I don't have to take shit from you. Get me? You and your—your—you know, if you hadn't been trying to play Mr. Hot Shot all night, none of this would've happened. We didn't have to stay 'round here all this time, I bet. I bet—"

"What do you know? *I* got the orders. I know what I'm doing."

"Well, all I can say is you sure ain't minded hot-shotting it around, having yourself the time of—"

"What about you?"

"Me? Don't be putting blame on me! Every time something goes wrong, you try to—"

"Aw, shut your trap."

Hedda scooped up a pack of cigarettes from the coffee table and managed to say even as she lit her cigarette, "And for the last time, don't be telling me to shut up, you hear?"

"Go fuck off, will you?" Fargo said, wondering what she was reaching for under the coffee table. "You're just like some—what's that?"

"It came out from your pants pocket when you was —" She stopped talking as he came nearer. She began spreading it out, fingering it. "It looks like—lorrrd, it looks like—"

"Give that here!" He snatched it. He almost dropped it. "It's—it's a handkerchief."

Hedda's eyelids opened wider. "I never seen a hanky yet that looked like woman's drawers." She leaned forward, her hands on her thin thighs. "Silk pants!"

Fargo flipped up the cloth quickly and stuffed it into his hip pocket. "A handkerchief, for Christ's sake." He put it in the wrong pocket; the black notebook kept it from going all the way in; it was bulging. "Silk handerkerchief," he muttered.

Hedda laughed so loud Fargo thought it would bring Cheeter back into the house. "Handerkerchief, my ass." Her hazel eyes began to sparkle and she spoke in mean little jabs. "I know pants when I see 'em. Woman's pants. Think I don't know, don't you? Baby, look. . . ." She walked back and forth, her arms folded, full of satisfaction. "If that's your kick, that's your business, that's your bag, but don't tell me that that there funky rag is a handkerchief when I know—"

"It's a handkerchief, Hedda! Why're you always trying to make something outta something that—"

"Prove it! Prove it, Mr. Hot Shot!" She rocked on her heels and stared him dead in the face. "Everybody knows about your sniffing kick, honey. If you want to sniff women's funky drawers, *sniff* women's funky drawers. Ain't nobody's problem but yours, but—don't you hit me, Fargo," she said, backing away as he raised his hand. "Don't you dare hit me! I ain't—ain't trying to meddle in your private business, but there ain't no point in calling me a liar when I know what I know. Unh-uh, not when I know what I know."

"You don't know shit."

"Yeah?" She leaned on the edge of the card table. "Whose *are* those? Did you snatch Sophie's panties when you went up to her room? Huh, Fargo?" Although her teeth snapped like a shark's, it looked as if she had tears in her eyes. "Or do you carry a supply around with you?"

He wasn't going to get excited and hit her. He wasn't going to stutter. They were all focusing on him. He could hear Cheeter whistling and he could hear the wind at the bay window. He wasn't going to—

"Huh, Fargo?"

"You're lying, Hedda." He looked at Finley, then at

Sophie and Olga. "Hedda's lying—talking dirty." When
nobody said anything, he added, "I mean, like you can
see how all that gin has gone to her head and it makes
her evil mouth go—"

Hedda sprang up and pulled whatever it was from
Fargo's back pocket. While his back was to her, ex-
plaining, she jerked it out. She flung it around in the
air. "Lie? Lie? Who's the liar?"

Fargo had not realized he'd pulled out his knife until
the blade hung there below Hedda's nose. The display
of the blade had put him in a corner, sticking it in her
face like that; he'd come on too strong, he couldn't lie
anymore. So, there it was. He did grab back the silk
panties, though, and he did hit her about the face a
couple of times, but there it was. He felt like a fool with
his knife in one hand and the panties in the other hand,
standing in the middle of the room while everybody
looked at him. Nobody laughed, but they looked at him
standing with the panties in one hand and the switchblade in the other, and from what he could see of his
face in the mirror across the room, nothing pleased him.
He was taller than he wanted to be. He was taking up
too much space, holding the knife and the panties in
his hands. Lord Jesus, what was he going to do with his
hands? The panties and the knife looked so small in his
big hands, so small, and he stood there unable to take
the panties and the knife out of his hands. Even the

horses at the fireplace—they were watching, looking at him, their porcelain tongues and porcelain eyes glistening at the fireplace with no fire in the fireplace.

How had Hedda known? From Benny or Cheeter? But how would *they* know? Maybe word got around; maybe big-mouthed Maurice had said something—but it wasn't likely they would know Maurice; Maurice, of West End Avenue, belonged to another world. . . .

Fargo had once bunked with Maurice for a few weeks —with Maurice who lived alone and made a lot of money. Fargo had just been kicked out of the small pad on West Twenty-second Street—from Cora's; Cora, an NYU student who had been less than a love affair but more than just a lay. Cora had gotten tired of him, or found a new lover, or both. On the Saturday morning she threw him out, he bumped into Maurice on the IND, at 6 a.m., at Columbus Circle, and Maurice suggested that he move in with him.

But how was he to know that the cat had that—that *affliction,* that hangup? In the army, where he first knew Maurice, in the paratroopers, Maurice hadn't; he was regular, and used to booze it up like the rest of them, and was one of the biggest cunt-hounds in Fort Benning. But after the first night he stayed with him, or maybe the second night, Fargo found out Maurice had changed. But maybe it was partly his own fault, too; he probably shouldn't have lost his head that night and taken Cora's panties out of his grip and—well, he *was* out of his mind about losing the bitch—and beating his meat with her panties over his face. The first time he did it, on Maurice's foldaway couch, tears, like some goddamn baby, came running down the sides of his cheeks in the dark, but he was careful not to get Maurice's sheets full of come. Maurice was neat about things.

But the second night, he didn't cry; it was all right—almost; he jerked off, and it seemed like he came for *days*, but Maurice must have heard, must've come out from his bedroom door and watched him there in the dark, because later on, a couple of days later, Fargo couldn't find the panties anywhere. He was ashamed to ask Maurice about them and at the same time he knew Maurice must have done something to them. And he had.

The next afternoon Fargo found them back in the bureau he was using—but washed, all neat and clean. It was only after threatening to beat the shit out of the bastard that the bastard owned up to the truth. Maurice said he'd taken them down to the laundromat; he'd had them washed with his own socks and towels. Maurice admitted he was jealous, admitted he'd watched Fargo from his bedroom door in the dark, beating his own meat off on the sly. Big tough-looking Maurice, with the heart of a woman underneath all that hair on his chest.

But he wasn't no fool, Maurice; Maurice said, put out or get out. Fargo got out. He got a room on West Eighty-third Street. Worse than the one he'd had before he shacked up with Cora. But they—Hedda, Cheeter, Benny—none of them knew Maurice. So how could they have known? Well, it wasn't none of their business. None of their business. . . .

"It's nobody's business, it's nobody's business," he said aloud, before he knew he was speaking, before he could think of a way to get out of it. "It's none of your fucking business," he told them, talking on, talking fast, hoping he'd stop looking so tall and so stupid in the middle of the room with his knife in his hand and with the damn panties in his hand. "It's—it's—all right, shit, this is my goddamn bag. So what if I sniff panties. So what! Ain't no law against it! You can't be put in jail for it! And—and—freaky? Fuck, the whole world's freaky. Ain't nobody so high up they don't do something freaky. Y'awl don't need to look like you gonna have some goddamn stroke or something. You hear? 'Cause, baby, all y'awl are in your goddamn bushwa bag, which is freaky in *my* books—with your white-folks talk and your white-folks ways and your turning your back on the race. And —and—"

"Course it's your business," Hedda said, looking smug and satisfied and evil, "but it's mighty funny they're bushwa panties. Like, explain away them apples, Mr.

Hot Shot. Huh? Bushwa panties with bushwa funk in 'em."

Fargo took a step toward Hedda.

Hedda went to the other side of the card table out of his reach. "Don't you lay a hand on me, Fargo. I swear I'll ram this here ashtray straight through your fucking skull."

"I—goddamn you, Hedda."

"Black bushwa panties, huh? That your kick?" With the metal ashtray tight in her hand, she said, "Them Sophie's panties? You steal 'em out of Sophie's room?"

"You foul-mouthed bitch."

"Never you mind my mouth—it's your fucked-up head I'm talkin' 'bout. How in the hell did the Committee make you in charge is what I want to know. *I* ought to've been in charge," she said, "not *you*."

Fargo sat on the sofa. Near Sophie. His legs didn't feel strong. He still had Sophie's panties in one hand, the knife in the other. He knew he ought to get rid of both. The knife cut no ice with Hedda; her viper tongue wouldn't be stopped. And what would he do with the pants now that he was caught with them, now that he'd held them in his hand so long? Throw them to the floor? Sling them on the coffee table? Return them to Sophie? Indecision made his hand tremble. They waited. All of them waited. The wind was getting so loud it was now making zizzling sounds. He felt naked.

"That's right, smell 'em, baby." Hedda was strutting. She grabbed somebody's warm gin, maybe her own, and swallowed it in one gulp. "Show Mama how you sniff them funky bushwa pants. Come on, show me. Show me. You ain't going to sniff for Mama? No?" She put the glass down, her chin high, triumphant. "You goddamn fucked-up coward! You phony! You coward! You freaky, phony coward! Lorrr-rrd, have mercy!"

Just as he dumped the pants on the coffee table in front of his knees, Sophie said, "Oh no," and began laughing. It got out of hand. She seemed to be having a hard time getting breath and she leaned her head on the back of the sofa and pressed her sides and said "Oh no" whenever she could speak. "My—my . . . panties . . ." She sounded as if she had asthma. She rolled her head from side to side, wheezing, laughing, making him feel like he had hives all over, like fast hot needles were being stuck up and down his back.

Fargo dropped the knife on the rug at his foot and picked up the pants from the coffee table. "You think it's funny, do you, bitch?" He took the panties and smashed them square over her laughing mouth, over her nose, pressing the silk cloth down hard. She squirmed. She stopped laughing. He was on top of her, one leg on the table, one leg under the table, smothering her with the garment and smothering her with his dashiki and his khaki trousers and pressing her deep into the cushions of the sofa. "You think it's funny, don't you?" She made no sound, but she stopped squirming, and he took the silk away from her face. He remained there, though, on top of her, tired, tired like he'd never before been tired, and watched her frown-up at the corners of her mouth as she stared back at him.

Fargo didn't know how long he lay there sprawled on top of her. The silk panties had fallen over the sofa arm into the magazine rack and the noise of the wind in the trees had faded away; he heard only the sound of her breathing, a muffled cotton-sound in the folds of his dashiki. He intended to move, any minute he would move away, for it seemed he'd lain there listening to her breathe for a long time.

Then when her breathing stopped coming in jerks, and sounded even again, she said, "Get off me."

He continued to lie there, talking to her mouth, which smelled of sherry. "You thought it was—you thought it was funny."

"Get off me."

"Didn't you?"

"Get off."

"Didn't you?"

"Your ear is cut."

"I know."

"It's cut bad."

"Yeah."

"I'm not sorry."

"I know."

"It may get infected."

"Maybe."

"But it's very bad. The cut. It is."

"Is it?"

"Does it hurt?"

"I don't know."

"Get off me."

"I will."

"Please, Fargo."

"I will."

"It's——" She traced a crusty line of dried blood over the lobe of his ear with the tip of her finger. "I'm not sorry. I'm not sorry at all."

"I know."

"But I'm not."

"I believe you."

"Fargo."

Then he slid off her, to the other side of the sofa, laying his head on the back of the sofa, with one leg on the coffee table and one leg under the coffee table. He was tired. But it was a good tired. Every muscle seemed at ease, tired, but at ease, and the flesh at the back of his knees felt—he felt like he'd just smoked grass. He felt giddy and he knew it was not from the scotch; the scotch had burnt up inside of him, had worn away.

He lay there and looked at the curlicues on the ceiling. Time was short. Twelve o'clock was but minutes away.

Fargo had to concentrate. It was necessary to concentrate. He must not not want twelve to come. . . . He must not not.

(8)

OLGA HAD closed her eyes to blot out Fargo's behavior—his long-legged straddle over Sophie—and she reminded herself that Sophie was still almost a child, not yet eighteen, and he, obviously some sort of oversexed brute, was at least twenty-seven or twenty-eight, a man. Certainly if lust was driving him, it would be directed toward a woman, and not to Sophie, nearly a child.

Yet her reasoning did little good, and she finally gave in: she was jealous, if only in theory, of Sophie and Fargo. Then suddenly she realized she'd been plain jealous of Sophie for a long time—jealous of her youth, of all the promise that lay ahead. Instead of being pleased with the knowledge that Sophie could use her youth at leisure, and luxuriate in it in a way she herself had not been able to do, Olga had all these years resented it. Secretly resented it. Bitterly resented it.

She flagellated herself with this truth, over and over, as if in some way she might make amends.

Then she opened her eyes.

Hedda was looking at her, but Hedda quickly turned her head away when Olga caught her glance.

Olga's heart beat faster. At last she was going to get inside Hedda's defense. At last. "Quite extraordinary that little scene, wasn't it, my dear?" Olga's voice was clear and strong. She moistened her lips. "Hmm?"

Hedda jerked to attention and smashed out her cigarette on Olga's rug.

But Olga would not, as much as she wanted to, look down at the ashy stub. "Hmm?" Olga said again.

"Watch out, honey," Hedda muttered. "I'm in no mood for any shit, you hear?"

Olga massaged her fingers and smiled. "I know facts are hard, but facts usually are, aren't they? I mean—"

Hedda jumped up and came toward Olga. Her hand was raised but she did not strike. "I told you, I'm in no mood for your shit!"

Olga did not move, or even flinch. She braced herself for a slap across the face and held her jaw firm. "Are you going to strike me again?"

For the first time that evening Hedda seemed to be lost and unsure of herself. She looked at Fargo and Sophie on the sofa and then turned back to Olga. Her lips twitched nervously as her hands groped for some imaginary object in the air. "I—I—" she stuttered, and then suddenly, as though she'd been plugged into an electric socket, her face became bright with malice.

Sharp sparkles filled her hazel eyes and her sullen mouth parted into a jagged smile. She'd found her weapon—her appropriate weapon, her smile seemed to say. As she walked toward Finley, she said, "Let's see who else can stage a little scene."

Olga froze. She'd not counted on this.

Hedda, her breath heavy with the odor of gin, began pulling and sliding Finley's chair across the room toward the study. "Me and him," she said, "are gonna take care of business."

"Oh, for God's sake, come on, now," Finley pleaded, trying to get a toehold in the rug. "Let's stop this—"

"You wouldn't!" Olga said, pressing her hands to her throat, staring in disbelief.

"Only if he can't get it up, I wouldn't."

Fargo stood. "Hedda!"

"What?" She paused. "Now you sit your black ass back down." She began pulling Finley toward the study again. "What's good for the gander is good for the goose. Huh, Fargo?"

"Don't," Fargo said, stammering, "don't untie him."

"Untie him?" Hedda said, just as she got Finley to the study door, "I ain't gonna untie him, I'm gonna fuck him—if he can get it up."

Hedda slammed the door.

The ceiling spun around and Teddy jumped upon the bay window seats and the porcelain horses galloped away from the fireplace. The wind made the vermilion sash at the velvet drapes prance. *It's not going to do you any good! It's not going to do you any good! He hasn't done anything in two years!* The china pieces sat on the table and clattered, bruising the spoons in unison.

At the door she pounded, but of course it was locked, and she crunched a piece of glass underfoot. Where was her other shoe? One shoe was on and one shoe was off, and where was her other shoe? *Two years! It's been two years! Two! Two! I tell you!* Teddy played the piano and his pink eyes blinked at pieces by Liszt. The decanters huddled together in preparation for a march.

All right, all right, let them be in there, let them be in there! Her knitting wobbled across the stones of the hearth. *Do I care? Do I care? I don't care! I don't care!* She must dance. But no one could dance with one shoe on and one shoe off. Could anyone dance with one shoe on and one shoe off? Fargo! Where was Fargo? There was a high necessity to dance. *Where is my shoe? Where is my shoe? You think I care? Let them be in there. Let them. I'll dance. I—*

With tentative, embarrassed gestures, Sophie tried to guide Olga to a seat. "Sit down, Mother. Please, sit down."

Fargo seemed embarrassed, too. His large hand almost touched Olga's shoulder in an effort toward tenderness.

"Look, Olga, you ought to—"

"Where's my shoe?"

"*Please,* Mother."

"Shoe, shoe, who stole my shoe?"

"You think you oughta get some coffee for her, Sophie?" Fargo asked.

"Who's the rat who stole my shoe? Who's the rat who—"

"Please, Mother, sit down."

"*Sit down?* I've got all my life to sit down. . . . I . . . now, where's my . . ."

"Oh, Mother, I *knew* this would happen. We *told* you not to—"

"Not to drink? Not to drink? That woman's in there with your—oh, get away, get away, that's just what I *am* going to shoe—do."

"Let her. Let her drink, Sophie," Fargo said. "Maybe she'll pass out again. It'll be better."

"I heard that, Fargo." Olga was, seemingly, almost sober again. "Oh, Fargo—where's the brandy? Who stole the brandy? Who—"

The thick liquid burned rivulets down her throat. And *see*—the sillies—it did not make her pass out. The heat of the liquid, the medicine in it, was stopping the ceiling from spinning and Teddy was leaving the piano and the sash was stopping its prancing and the spoons were stopping their clattering and . . . but she still did not have her shoe. The glass moons of the china cabinet stared at her foot until she knew exactly what to do. She took it off, her other shoe. She took it off. *Play,*

*Sophie. Let's have music. We need music. Play, for
God's sake, Sophie, play. Fargo and I are going to
dance. . . .*

She'd fallen into Fargo and found herself squeezing
his shoulder and counting the ribs along his back.
"Hmm, Fargo?" Then, across his shoulder, she saw her
shoe. Her missing shoe. There by her Bloomingdale
lamp. How did her shoe get—then she heard that laugh,
that hyena laugh from behind the study door.

Bitch! Olga broke away from Fargo and shouted at
the study door with all the force she had. "You dirty,
rotten bitch! I hope you burn in hell! Eternal hell!"

There was silence from the study. Not a sound. Then
Sophie said, pacing the floor, "For crissake, Mother,
don't descend to *her* level. There's nothing to be done."

"What? What?" Olga turned on Sophie. She wanted
to run to her, fall into her arms, ask her to forgive her,
but out of seventeen years of habit, out of mutilated
pride, the words that came were the same old words,
with the same willful destruction beaded into them. She
wanted to say, "Sophie, please show me how to love
you"; she said instead, "How dare you turn on me this
way! *You, too?* Go—go play with Teddy or something,
for God's sake." A sneering smile crossed her face, but
she'd not known how to stop it.

Sophie looked as if she were on the verge of a tantrum,
a nervous breakdown, or worse. Olga had never seen her

daughter's face so distorted. Sophie's hands, in small fists, were poised, ready to smash anything in sight. She turned toward the mantel. She turned toward the liquor cabinet. She rushed past Fargo, past the study door into the kitchen. She rattled among the forks and spoons. When she came running out, her fists still in tight knots, she seemed to be demented, turning right and left, and then, at the foot of the coffee table, where Fargo had dropped her panties, she found what her frenzy needed: Fargo's switchblade knife. For an awful moment, Olga thought Sophie would plunge the blade into her throat, into her breast, for the hatred in her eyes was immense. Her round-rimmed glasses had fallen to the floor. Crouched like an animal, she clutched the knife until it seemed the bones of her knuckles would break through the flesh; she looked as if she might be about to plunge the blade into her own stomach in some violent hara-kiri. Olga froze. But Sophie's fury was not directed against herself. She found her object: Teddy.

Sophie plunged the long blade into Teddy's belly, over and over, raising it as high as her head and bringing the blade down each time in a new death. The power of her thrust was such that her hand was driven down over the knife's guard and the blade ate quickly across the inside of her hand. A gush of blood poured through her fingers and, when she raised her hand to look at it, ran down her wrist.

Sophie looked at her hand in a daze, almost objectively, as if it were not her hand but someone else's.

"It's—it's bleeding," she said, looking at it in amazement. She took a few uncertain steps, the blood spilling to the rug, and said, "I'm bleeding."

Fargo went to her. "You—you stabbed Teddy."

"I'm bleeding."

He took Sophie's hand, quietly, and in a strange slow motion placed it upon his black skin. He moved her hand gently, slowly, pressing the blood upon his cheek, across his lips, over his nose. Slowly.

Just as Olga shut her eyes to the sight of the bloody tenderness upon Fargo's face, she heard Hedda's laughter from behind the study door.

Nothing mattered now. Anything—anything—would be a relief.

She plunged into Fargo, her hands in small hard claws, with no plan. The frenzied tearing at his dashiki and torso was only mindless action, somehow preferable to silent despair. She had no plan. Her thrusts of clawed anger at Fargo were really meant for Hedda. She shivered with hate and embarrassment as she remembered what she had perhaps said about Finley. She pummeled Fargo until one of her frantic tearing hands came by chance upon the pistol butt. Her fingers closed over it and she suddenly backed away. With the gun in her hand, she stood trembling, frowning, frightened.

Fargo made a move to take the weapon from her but

Olga stepped back, panting, and began to wave the gun to and fro in front of her face.

Her insane carelessness, the lack of caution with the lethal weapon, unnerved Fargo. He backed away. He tried to smile as he held on to the edge of Finley's easy chair, as though he might any minute duck behind it. "Come on, please," he said. "You can—can get hurt— it might go off." He stuttered and the gleam of sweat mingled with the blood on his face.

Olga had no plan. She only knew she must act, act in some way, but she had no plan. She looked at the gun, turning its muzzle to her nose, as if she might smell it. Sophie, seeing the gun turned toward Olga's own face, said, "No, Mama! Please, no!"

Olga's mind registered dimly that Sophie had called her "Mama," but she was beyond understanding the unexpected love in the word, just as she was beyond rational thinking. Despair was driving her toward some final act. An act of destruction. Complete destruction. There must be no halfway measures, no sloppiness, no failure.

Fargo got closer to the back of the easy chair.

Sophie stood still, pain cut across her lips.

Olga, with her arm extended rigidly in front of her as though she were a marksman on a firing range, slowly pointed the gun at Fargo. He quickly ducked behind Finley's easy chair.

Olga slowly swung the gun to Sophie. She pinched her lips and stood her ground, glaring.

Olga pointed the gun to the study door and held it pointed at the door for a long time. A tear fell, rolled down her cheek, and clung at the edge of her chin.

Next she moved the gun to Teddy. The switchblade was still lodged in his belly.

And then, whether she meant to, or whether it was an accident—even later she never quite knew—she pointed the pistol at the piano.

She fired. The pistol fire eased some of her tension, eased some of her anger. With her hair in her face, her arm extended rigidly, her eyes closed tightly, she fired again and again and again, emptying the bullets into the piano.

Keys split and bullets ricocheted—one chipped the top of a horse's head at the fireplace, another cracked a pane in the china closet. There was the smell of gunpowder. There were echoes in the silence.

Even after Olga had emptied the barrel, she continued to hold the gun rigidly outward, toward the piano. Her eyes were still closed. Even as Hedda ran into the room, as Cheeter appeared at the front door, her eyes were still closed.

"What the—!" Hedda said.

"What the fuck—!" Cheeter said.

"Olga?" Finley called from the study.

Olga dropped the pistol on the rug and opened her eyes. The sight of Hedda dressed in Olga's magenta housecoat jolted her from her murderous reverie.

The sight of Cheeter with his gun stung her to life.

She beat her fist into her palm and said to Cheeter in a hoarse whisper, "So? . . . so, for God's sake, use it, use it." She said again, rasping and thick, "Go ahead, shoot!"

"Olga!" Finley shouted from the study, scraping his chair across the floor, attempting to get into the living room. "Hey, out there!"

Cheeter, with his sunglasses on, seemed confused. He held the gun in front of him as though it were a hot-handled skillet. His shaven head was wet with sweat.

Then Olga's hard tranquillity broke and she began to sob in chokes and jerks. She fell to her knees before Cheeter, crying in deep-throated bronchial rasps, pounding the rug at her knees, pounding the rug in front of Cheeter's feet. Even her destruction, like everything else in her life, would be a failure, would not be complete. She made one last attempt: from her knees she looked up at Cheeter, her face twisted, her lip curled downward, a string of saliva dripping from her snarled lip, and screamed: "Kill me! Kill me! Kill me!" She touched the spot on her forehead where she wanted the bullet.

Cheeter backed away. His jaw shook. He backed away. He wiped sweat from the surface of his sunglasses.

Olga stayed on her knees, her hands now hanging limply at her sides, her head bowed, as if in penance for her sins. She'd stopped crying.

Then, through the opened door, from a block away, came shouts: "At the Blakes'! At Finley Blake's!" Porch lights went on. Garage lights went on. Somewhere in the night, doors opened and shut. In the distance, there was a siren. And upstairs, Sybil Sykes' voice was calling, "Help us, somebody! Help us!"

Cheeter dashed out the front door and down the lawn.

"Oh, Christ," Fargo said. "Let's haul ass!"

Hedda grabbed Fargo's arm.

Olga raised her head in time to see Fargo streaking across the lawn. Hedda's long legs were not far behind.

"Olga!" Finley shouted. "What's going—"

"Finley! Olga!" Someone was shouting from the end of the lawn near the cedar gate. It sounded like Marvin Bercowitz, their nearest neighbor. More porch lights went on. The dark night was now lit up in splashes of bluish-grays, and there was the sound of running feet from all directions.

Then the phone rang.

The shrill sound ate into the stale air of the room. It was a minute before twelve.

Olga rose. Calmly. Spent and numb, she picked up the receiver and said immediately, before any voice spoke, "They are not here." She paused, caught her breath, and said, with stark finality, "They will not be back."

She replaced the phone, having not heard a single word from the caller, and walked—one slow step after another—erectly up the stairs.

It took her a long time to get to her bedroom. Each step upward was an effort. All her attention was directed to one step after another, upward, even though many things began to happen about her. People appeared at the downstairs door. The siren grew louder. Sophie untied Finley. By the time Olga made it to her room there seemed to be a dozen people hovering at her opened door, but she was not sure, for she did not look up from her mirror where at long last she was able to apply to her face the soothing balm of Nutrea 7.

No one came in. They stood—all of them—watching her. She did not look at their faces. She needed her remaining strength for her task at the dresser: one glance, one word would only be a waste of her dwindling energy.

As she carefully wiped away the excess lotion with a tissue, the red swirling light of a police car in the driveway made carousel shadows on the wallpaper. She thought she heard Finley call out to her from the hallway, and she thought she saw Sybil Sykes gently restrain him from entering her bedroom, but she could not be sure, for there was a crowd of people now, many people, and their voices and faces blended, faded and blended.

She wiped away a streak of Nutrea 7 from her finger. She got up from her dresser. She headed toward her bed. She was just two steps away from it when she fainted and fell to the floor.

(Tuesday, March 11)

A B O U T S I X months after the metropolitan newspapers garbled the story of the Blakes' intruders in St. Albans (among other inaccuracies, Olga was called a heroine, having—one reporter said—wrested a revolver, single-handed, from one of the thugs and chased them all out of the house with gunfire), Olga saw Fargo. She was sitting in Morningside Park. Just before sundown.

Olga had taken to stopping in the park after her Tuesday and Thursday voluntary work at the West Harlem Day Center. She used to reread Sophie's letters from Bennington there in the park. Sophie had written that she was pleased that Olga had taken the job working with underprivileged children. Early in October, Olga had written back that she was pleased, too. That started it—their correspondence.

Now they each wrote two letters a week, using the mails to establish and confirm their new relationship. At first, they had written cautiously, a little stiffly, feeling each other out, but gradually the letters became warmer, freer. Sophie repeatedly spoke of Olga's "courage and bravery" on that night of the intruders. Olga knew better: she'd been driven to despair, and her courageous act (as the newspaper account had described it, too) was motivated by fear and remorse. But must she, Olga reasoned, disillusion so many people? After all, some good was coming out of it—at least it was healing the wounds between her and her daughter.

Recently, however, Olga had become apprehensive: would the newly found warmth and cordiality that filled their letters disappear when Sophie, at Easter vacation, came home? Yet . . . maybe it would be all right, for Sophie had expressed much the same fear in a recent letter. This, Olga decided, was a good omen—if they both were afraid of meeting each other, a new beginning might be possible.

But it was not Sophie's most recent letter that Olga carried around in her purse; it was Sophie's February 5 letter that, in some odd and indefinable way, offered the greatest comfort, gave her the greatest warmth. (Characteristically, Sophie had dated it "Feb. 5 or 6"; they were nearly all like that—"Jan. 21 or 22"—"Tuesday, or is it Wednesday?" Really, Olga thought with fond amusement, how can the child get to her classes if she doesn't even know what day it is! And characteristically too, Sophie's February 5 letter started out with an apology and reference to her refusal to come home during her vacation at Christmastime.)

Olga slowly fingered through the letter again, although she knew nearly every line by heart. . . .

. . . *Because I had to find myself, you know? I mean,
Daddy seemed more irked about my not coming
home last Christmas than you did—at least in that
one little old stingy letter he wrote I thought so.
Anyway, Katie and I had a super time in Syracuse—
even if it was eternally 4 or 5 above zero. But I've
said all this before—what I want to tell you is—well,
Mother, sit down while you read this—I have some
NEWS. It's really spooky. Crazy. Are you ready? I
saw Fargo last week! No, no, don't get jittery and
everything—nothing happened—I mean, we didn't
even speak.*

*Look, do understand, now. I didn't tell you right
off because I wasn't sure if I'd done the right thing,
and if I hadn't done the right thing, why hadn't I,
and what was the right thing, anyway? I've kept asking
myself that ever since. Sorry, I'm not making sense,
am I? It was like this: you remember I told you about
the Students for Relevant Action group I got in-
volved with? You know with the series of speakers
we've been having since November like Eric Lauder;
whatshisname from California—the socialist newspaper man I thought a bit of an ass; Father Crakye,
etc. You remember, don't you? Well, I had to put
my 2 cents worth in and asked the selection committee
why didn't we have a black speaker for a change.
Katie, who is about as WASP as you can get, was all
for it too—(though, dear heart that she is, she's a*

*mite naïve—can you imagine—she was ready to pick
up the phone to call Julian Bond to come to talk—
for a measly $350—I'm sure he wouldn't even come
for our top price of $500).*

*Anyway, Mother, after much hassling, we decided
(rather* they *did because I'd never heard of the man
before) on Mitchell Lewis who was described as
being somewhere between Martin Luther King and
Eldridge Cleaver. (Didn't* that *tell me a lot? I mean,
it's like telling someone this or that composer is
somewhere between Vivaldi and John Cage!!) Anyway, I went along with it. Lewis is out of (or was, I
guess) Pittsburgh. Edits a magazine (I've not seen)
called Ododo—which means truth, I think. Or does
it mean faith? Anyhow . . . Mary Beacom and
Donna Walker and a couple of other kids were on
the social committee so I didn't see Mitchell Lewis
until he was already up there on the stage. (I had
this stupid French paper to finish and couldn't have
been with them had I wanted.) But guess what? Bigger
than life, with all six-feet-something of his body
stuffed into a dark green dashiki and gray trousers
sat—yep, Fargo. And as some sort of bodyguard!! Can
you imagine how I felt? I didn't know whether to
run for the police or sit there and cry. I felt dizzy and
nearly ready to throw up—yet, I was fascinated, too.
Fargo looked so—so, I don't know, sort of vulnerable
and pathetic in spite of his self-important air. He*

didn't say a word, of course. Just sat there on the podium next to Mitchell Lewis. It's a wonder I heard a single word. My head was swimming. I couldn't take my eyes off him—even when I imagined he spied me in the audience (it was a smallish room, less than 400 students and faculty).

Oh, Mother, it was awful—I couldn't go out and I couldn't sit there—I don't know how I got through that hour and twenty minutes. The 20 minutes was question and answer time. I couldn't have asked a question for all the rubies at Tiffany's. Anyway, what little I did hear from Lewis's talk was hogwash as far as I'm concerned . . . that old tiresome line . . . "blacks aren't individuals, they are part of a cause" and stuff like "art must support the black revolution; if it doesn't, it's invalid," etc. Professor Baugh in my history class says the Russians said the same thing about their revolution in 1917.

Anyway—Katie dragged me along to the reception room for cake and coffee—I was so numb I couldn't beg out—and when I went to shake hands with Lewis, Fargo must have seen me for the first time. He stood next to Lewis with such a look in his eyes—sort of pleading—like he was saying "please don't tell"— and when I moved on to get coffee and cake (you think I could even open my mouth [?!?]—not to speak of eating anything), I thought he bowed his head

*just the tiniest bit as if he was saying "thanks" or
something.*

*Mother, what should I have done? I mean, he did
look so sad and scared and, you know, in a funny way,
sort of gentle. I mean, what could the dean have
done anyway—I mean, had I told, or said something?
Or the police? I mean, he could have denied it all
right there on the spot. But what really bothers me
is that I didn't want to do anything. Do you
understand? I really didn't want to do anything.*

*It's been awful these days—keeping this all to
myself—I didn't even tell Katie. And please, please,
don't tell Daddy. I mean, I feel like a fool about it
and I had to tell somebody, and it's been—well, will
you promise not to tell Daddy? I've first got to
straighten the whole thing out in my mind. Promise?*

*The crocheted hat fits perfectly and it is warm as
you said it'd be, but Mother—now don't get angry—
it's really not me—I mean, the color is wrong—to
be honest, I don't like it all that much—Katie thinks
it is super—may I give it to her?*

Must dash off to a dreary Poli Sci thing. More later.

Love, Sophie

Sophie's letter was dogeared as much from Olga's
constant rereading of it as it was from being changed
from purse to purse. She did not dare to leave it around

the house—not that Finley was a snoop—but there'd been for a time a silly mix-up of keys. The entire house, as Finley had insisted, now had new locks on the doors. Unfortunately, the wretched keys to the old locks had not been thrown away. New keys and old keys were jumbled together, and on more than one occasion, Finley muttered and cursed as he pawed around in drawers in search of this or that key. Although Olga was sure the Great Key Confusion was pretty well resolved and that he wasn't likely to continue his search, she still would not chance leaving Sophie's February 5 letter around. If he *did* come across it, he surely would read it and carelessness would be tantamount to treachery. Moreover, the letter brought great warmth to Olga: the complicity, no matter how insignificant in essence, was, Olga felt, the surest sign of the growing trust between them. Olga sometimes muttered aloud, while walking through Lord & Taylor's or while rinsing out her nylons, *Sophie, you may tell Finley if you wish, but I never will.* This resolution made her smile.

She had been smiling quite a bit these days apparently, even without realizing it; even Sybil had noticed and remarked, "Darling, I know the expression is 'grinning like a Cheshire cat,' but all evening you've been smiling like one." Ostensibly, Sybil had come up the road to borrow some crème de menthe to make stingers, but Olga knew very well it was merely to gossip. (There was a rumor that Marvin and Ruthie Bercowitz were planning a trial separation.) "Smiling?" Olga asked, picking through the bottles on the liquor cabinet as she hunted for the crème de menthe. "Was I smiling?" It was the third time within two and a half hours she'd tried to send Sybil on her way. "Ah, here, but it's not much," Olga said, picking up the bottle. "We've a lot of green chartreuse. Won't that do as well?"

Sybil turned her back on the proffered bottles and plopped down in Finley's easy chair, crossing her moth-gray pants-suit legs. "Come clean, love," she said to Olga. "What are you up to?"

Olga didn't want to play games with Sybil, and she knew that Sybil had been eyeing her curiously for some weeks now. But how was she to tell Sybil, dear flighty Sybil, what had happened to her, what was happening to her, when she herself hardly knew? Her only recourse was to pursue the obvious line. "Up to?" Olga said, returning from the cabinet to the sofa. "What do you mean? Sybil, you honestly don't think I'm just pretending about Marvin and Ruthie, do you? Really, I swear I haven't heard a thing."

Sybil flipped her purple glass beads back and forth with impatience. "Oh, the devil with Marvin and Ruthie. I can get all the dirt about those two from Maggie Coleman if I really want to."

Olga could not resist saying, "Well?" Some of her old iciness crept back into her voice, and hearing its haughty tonality, she thought: Strange, have I always sounded like that?

"Oh darling, come on," Sybil said, "you know what I mean."

"No, really. What? You said something about—"

"Well, for one thing," Sybil said in a rush of words pent up too long without airing, "you've stopped taking those diet pills—you're getting piggy-fat. Why?"

The accusation was only partly justified; true, Olga had put on eight pounds, and each pound showed, but hardly with pigginess. She gently pressed in her waist and suppressed a smile in fear it would further provoke Sybil. "Why not? *Harper's Bazaar* never chased after me even in my best years." Olga leaned back on the couch, loose-limbed, ungracefully, and added, "Anyway, I think Finley rather likes me this way."

"*Likes* you that way?" Sybil said incredulously.

"You know," Olga said, hoping her smile wasn't too smug, "a little something to hang on to."

"Olga, you're disgusting," Sybil said and quickly lit a cigarette. "I honestly don't understand you anymore. Are you in an old-age syndrome or something? Are you going through menopause?"

"Now, really, Sybil, come on," Olga said, not shifting from her sprawling position on the sofa.

"Well, what is it, then?" Sybil's freckles seemed to take fire. She leaned forward, thrusting her cigarette in Olga's direction as she spoke. "Take that Children's

Day Center thing. I mean, it's all terribly noble and stuff to work with poor kids, but—I suppose—I suppose you'll be a Gray Lady next!"

Olga felt she should answer, but it took too much energy. Besides, she wondered, how on earth would she reply?

"And what about The Tuesday Club?" Sybil asked.

"What about it?"

"I mean you're *never* there anymore. All the girls keep asking about you. The thing is, dozens and dozens would give all sorts of eyeteeth to belong and here you are—well, it is frightfully important, you must admit."

"Important? Oh, I suppose maybe . . ."

"Well, if not important, it's terribly *in*." Sybil turned sharply and faced Olga. "Now deny that. Just deny it."

Olga sat up and tried to pull herself together, to be kind to her visitor. But before she could think of a way to change the subject, Sybil was off again.

"And, darling, that hideous piano with all those bullets in it. Why in the devil don't you chuck it out?"

Olga gazed at the bullet-scarred spinet with its splintered keys. "Oh, I don't know," she said absently. "Anyway, it's just a piano."

"*Just a piano?*" Sybil said, whirling around on a purple vinyl shoe. "That hideous piece of rubbish? And all it reminds you of? Darling, what has gotten *into* you?"

"Now, now, Sybil," Olga said, her gaze still on the

spinet, "don't fuss—after all, it's just a piano—a dead piano, if you will, but I don't—"

"You're damned right, Olga, it's a dead piano, so why—"

"Don't *fuss,* Sybil. Really there's—"

"Who's fussing? I only said why keep it."

Sybil, Olga was shocked to see, was near to tears. She could only say to her distraught visitor, "But, why not?"

"Why not?" Sybil's voice rose hysterically. Her hand trembled. "Why not, you ask!"

"Yes," Olga said evenly, logically, "why not?"

"It's—it's . . ." Sybil turned sharply to douse her cigarette. In a jerky, hasty stretch, she picked up the crème de menthe bottle and said tightly, "Must run. Thanks awfully."

Olga stopped her at the foyer steps. "Sybil . . . hey . . . you aren't angry, are you?"

"Angry? Angry?" The freckles over her face sharpened into small dots. "Whatever on earth for?" She turned quickly, her beads clinking against the crème de menthe bottle, and hurried out the front door.

Poor Sybil, Olga thought. Had the piano caused her so much distress? She looked at the spinet for a long time, remembering the years of polish that had been applied to it, remembering Sophie's trials and joys upon its keys. Yes, it surely had had its day. Perhaps she ought to get rid of it, but why the rush? It was only an old piano, something of the past.

She sat down on the bench and poked a key. The wailing *ping* made her laugh. She put both hands on the keyboard and tried to remember a forgotten piece —a minuet—but the music rose in the room like a hurdy-gurdy at a carnival, as if to mock her past vanities, her past glories. And because the music sounded so grotesque, and because inexplicably she felt such a surge of liberation, an uncoiling, she sat there crying and laughing, laughing and crying, not caring that her fingers were hopelessly blundering over the splintered keys.

When she finished playing, she shook her head slowly from side to side. "Poor Sybil," she murmured. "Poor, dear Sybil."

So on Tuesday, March 11, Olga sat rereading Sophie's February letter in Morningside Park. It was a crisp day, dry and cold. If it had been a bit warmer, Olga would have killed time by staying there longer on the park bench and watching, as she usually did, the young boys with their football and the young girls with their roller skates. But despite the bright setting sun bathing her brown tweed coat, she thought she had better walk on up the hill to Columbia. She was auditing a course on Yucatan art. She had enrolled in the course not so much because it was of great interest to her but because the hours worked perfectly with her Tuesday and Thursday duty at the Harlem Day Center and with Finley's

Tuesday and Thursday hours at Mount Sinai. He would usually pick her up after the lecture and they often had dinner in Manhattan.

Olga had just wiggled her last finger into her amber glove when she saw him. Fargo! She'd never forget that walk. That swagger. At first, though, she thought it couldn't be he—he was just in her mind because of Sophie's letter, and besides, the sun was in her eyes, and this man was dressed so oddly—at least, she thought it was odd for Fargo. He wore some sort of uniform, such as a filling-station attendant might wear. Dark green. Baggy pants. And through his unzipped windbreaker, she saw on his chest a red circular emblem with a name stitched over it.

She barely breathed. He walked by. But he had seen her, surely, for the sun had not been in his eyes, and she was sure her appearance had not altered all that much during the last six months.

But it was he—unmistakably. He walked by without looking. Then, just as Olga had made sure her purse was fastened and had gathered up her notebook, he turned back. He came over to her bench. *He sat. Next to her.*

Olga held her breath. She looked straight ahead. The idea of jumping up and running struck her as ludicrous (it was still quite light out), yet sitting there, not speaking, was equally silly. But what was she to say? She thought of Sophie's panic. Even if she *had* something to say, she was certain she would not be able to get it out. Her mouth was as dry as sand.

He, too, sat there silently, looking straight ahead, not moving. In a short time, Olga sensed that there were to be no speeches, no talk between them. They sat there, tautly, on the bench, like two strangers sitting side by side at a movie.

As the sun began to sink over the hill at Morningside Drive, sink westward into the Hudson, the air became chillier. Somehow, though, she could not move. She felt, perhaps perversely, a bond with this man, with Fargo, now so ordinary—though still handsome—but now dressed so ordinarily in his—his—she was certain it was a gas-station suit. Now that there was a relaxed recognition (still silent) of each other's presence, she was almost tempted to look around at the crest on his shirt. But she did not have to. He smelled of oil. And his fingernails were dirty. What had happened to his role as bodyguard? *And he wore a ring.* Her heart took a jump. Was it a wedding ring, and if so, was it for Hedda?

Hedda. Olga tried to remember how much she'd feared and hated Hedda, but it didn't work. She could not dredge up that old hate and fear; she could scarcely remember it; she had perhaps purged herself more thoroughly than she realized on that night when she knelt before Cheeter.

Suddenly on impulse—because he looked so vulnerable, and ordinary, and smelled of oil—Olga dropped her gloved hand down on the bench, covering Fargo's fingers. She did not look at him as she did this, nor did he look at her. They both sat there, still as if in a movie, her amber-gloved fingers covering his large black hand, a hand now ashy from the cold air. Quietly and gently, Olga fingered his ring. She squeezed his fingers, removed her hand, and then stood up, keeping her gaze upon three boys with a hoop in the distance before her.

She walked away without looking back.

Although the zigzagged stone pathway up the park to Morningside Drive was treacherous in her thin shoes, she paid little attention to her feet; every now and then she would glance sideways, surreptitiously, at Fargo's large figure still sitting on the bench. The weak glare of the sun, fractured by early-spring branches, washed yellow zebra stripes over Fargo's uniform. In the distance, on her way up the hill, she turned and stopped. As she looked back at the leggy figure, just for one last look, he waved.

It had not been a wave exactly: he'd raised his arm and hand as if to caress a sun ray in the cold March air. Then he'd slowly dropped his hand back to the bench, bringing back from the air bits of the sun that had clung to the gold of his ring.

Olga waved quickly and went on up the hill to her Yucatan lecture at Columbia. .

After dinner, on Adelaide Lane, Olga sat on the sofa across from Finley and pretended to knit. They had not gone to Pierre au Tunnel as they'd planned because it had begun to snow, and parking would be a headache, and besides, she had a perfectly good roast at home.

As she adjusted her silver needles, she again pretended to knit, but she could not. She was happy. She couldn't knit when she was happy. Her fingers trembled.

"Finley," she said, "what do you think we ought to have in the way of food when Sophie comes?"

Finley was picking at a loose thread at the toe of his sock, reading a newspaper.

"Finley?"

"Hmm?"

"Sophie gets back week after next. Easter vacation. Now about food. What do you think?"

"That's nice."

Olga shrugged and decided he'd have no worthwhile suggestions anyway; he'd eat hamburger every night if it were left up to him. She then looked around the living room, wondering whether she ought to make a few changes before Sophie came, but on careful survey she decided there was really little she could do. The china closet occupied a great deal of space. And the piano. The teddy bear had been discarded, but the piano was still there. Oh, she could scarcely wait to see Sophie, to tell her that she, *too,* had seen Fargo! At last they really had something to share! But Finley— there was no reason he shouldn't know about *her* encounter.

"Finley," she said.

"Hmm?"

"Guess who I saw today? In the park. Guess."

Finley lowered his paper an inch and made a non-committal mumble.

"Fargo," she said. "Fargo Hurn. I saw him in the park. Quite by accident."

"That's nice."

Olga dropped her knitting and leaned back on the sofa. She laughed without making a sound, and rolled her head slowly from side to side. Finley, her Finley, would always be the same. Although they had once again taken to sleeping together, Finley, her Finley, would always be the same.

For a long time, with her head resting on the back of the sofa, Olga smiled at the newsprint hiding her husband's face.